"You are vulnerable, Mina. You are looking at me like I'm some knight who's come to your rescue when I am anything but. You have no idea what you are throwing out there right now."

She swallowed hard. "I *am* vulnerable right now but I *want* to feel vulnerable. I *want* to want what I want. I want to figure out who I am. And I am under no illusions as to what this would be between us. I've just said I'm not looking for a commitment. Not now. Not for a long while."

Nate was silent, so silent she could hear her heart pounding in her ears. "Just to be clear," he rasped finally, "you're telling me you want us to go to bed together. And to hell with the consequences?"

She bit the inside of her mouth. *Hard.* "You keep baiting me, Nate. You won't leave it alone, either. What do *you* want?"

The Billionaire's Legacy

A search for truth and the promise of passion!

For nearly sixty years, Italian billionaire
Giovanni Di Sione has kept a shocking secret.
Now, nearing the end of his days, he wants his
grandchildren to know their true heritage.

He sends them each on a journey to find his
"Lost Mistresses," a collection of love tokens—
the only remaining evidence of his lost identity,
his lost history...his lost love.

With each item collected the Di Sione siblings
take one step closer to the truth...
and embark on a passionate journey
that none could have expected!

Find out what happens in

The Billionaire's Legacy

Di Sione's Innocent Conquest by Carol Marinelli

The Di Sione Secret Baby by Maya Blake

To Blackmail a Di Sione by Rachael Thomas

The Return of the Di Sione Wife by Caitlin Crews

Di Sione's Virgin Mistress by Sharon Kendrick

A Di Sione for the Greek's Pleasure by Kate Hewitt

A Deal for the Di Sione Ring by Jennifer Hayward

The Last Di Sione Claims His Prize by Maisey Yates

Collect all eight volumes!

Jennifer Hayward

A DEAL FOR THE DI SIONE RING

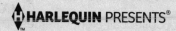
HARLEQUIN PRESENTS®

Recycling programs
for this product may
not exist in your area.

ISBN-13: 978-0-373-06029-0

A Deal for the Di Sione Ring

First North American Publication 2016

Copyright © 2016 by Harlequin Books S.A.

Special thanks and acknowledgment are given to Jennifer Hayward for her
contribution to The Billionaire's Legacy series.

Printed in U.S.A.

Jennifer Hayward has been a fan of romance since filching her sister's novels to escape her teenage angst. Her career in journalism and PR, including years of working alongside powerful, charismatic CEOs and traveling the world, has provided perfect fodder for the fast-paced, sexy stories she likes to write, always with a touch of humor. A native of Canada's East Coast, Jennifer lives in Toronto with her Viking husband and young Viking-in-training.

Books by Jennifer Hayward

Harlequin Presents

Kingdoms & Crowns

The Delicious De Campos

Visit Harlequin.com for more titles.

For Melody, who took me into the world
of ultra-luxury hotels and taught me what
a six-star property is, what a butler does
and why someday I must stay in one!
You are one of the special people.

And for my sister, Susan, a brilliant psychologist,
who helps me dig deep into the heads
of my characters. Thank you! Xx

CHAPTER ONE

THE WEALTH AND OPULENCE of Long Island's legendary Gold Coast was like a trip back in time to the old
money, scandalous, glamorous tales immortalized in
American fiction. High-society dynasties born of the
Industrial Revolution had built these lavish mansions
and castles one after another along this sweep of the
ruggedly beautiful northern coast, with gardens rival-
ing European grandeur.

They had sought to outdo one another, these American
scions, to glitter as the Gold Coast's preeminent jewel.
But as with so many other symbols of that lavish time,
little of the grandeur of those magnificent estates survived
today, with only a few of the massive, character-filled
mansions still left standing. Even legendary shipping
magnate Giovanni Di Sione's sprawling villa, built in
the late eighteen hundreds as a rambling summerhouse
to entertain the scion's clients and financiers, had been
extensively renovated to stand as a shining symbol of
modern architecture.

The ostentatious display of wealth, the almost tan-
gible scent of old money in the air, brought with it fa-

miliar irony for Nate Brunswick as he turned his Jaguar down the rolling, winding stretch of road toward the Di Sione estate. He could buy the Gold Coast several times over with the wealth he'd amassed and add it to the vast global property empire he controlled and still never feel like he belonged.

It was a lesson he'd learned the hard way. That all the money in the world couldn't heal old wounds. That new money would always be just that in New York— the spoils of an interloper who didn't really belong. New blood might mix with blue blood, but it would never have the same status in the collective psyche of the elite.

It was a truth he would put right up there with the Ten Commandments: *Thou shalt not aspire to join our realm. It has never been, nor will it ever be, yours.*

He brought the Jag to a halt in front of his grandfather's villa with a defiant squeal of its wheels. The villa's imposing facade gleamed in the late-afternoon sun, the light setting off its graceful arches and multileveled roofline.

He sat for a moment, a heavy weight pressing down on his chest. Always this place inspired a wealth of emotion, all of it complex and decades in the making. But today he felt as if whatever higher power was up there in the sky orchestrating this chess game that was life had reached inside him and yanked out his heart.

His grandfather was dying of leukemia. Nate had been traveling so much of late, overseeing his sprawling, global property empire, he had had little time for his mentor, who had been the only father figure he'd ever known. He'd stood there, shell-shocked, as his half sister Natalia had told him at her art exhibition that his grandfather's leukemia was back, and this time, a bone marrow transplant from Nate would not save him.

Apparently not even the all-powerful Giovanni could cheat death twice.

The swell of emotion he'd been fighting during the drive from Manhattan swept over him, threatened to wipe away the composure he had cultivated as a second skin. He blinked and pushed it away. He would not allow that expression of weakness. Not now and definitely not here.

He swung his long legs out of the car, wincing as his muscles protested the long drive in the low-slung machine. He had barely put his foot on the top step of the sweeping column of stairs that led to the villa's elegant entrance when Alma, the Di Sione family's longtime housekeeper, opened the door.

"Master Nate," Alma greeted him, ushering him in. "Signor Giovanni is enjoying the last rays of the sun on the back veranda. He's been anxiously awaiting your arrival."

A twinge of guilt stirred low in his gut. He should have made more time for his grandfather, but he had fallen into the trap of thinking Giovanni was invincible like everyone else.

A few pleasantries exchanged with Alma, he set off toward the back of the villa, his footsteps echoing on the gleaming marble floors. He'd first visited this house at eighteen, hunted down by his half brother Alex as the only genetic match for a bone marrow transplant that would save his grandfather's life—a man Nate had never met.

A vision of his six half siblings perched on the hand-made wrought-iron and stone staircase filled his head. They had sat there, lined up like birds on a telephone wire, big eyes inquisitive as Alex had led Nate past them into the salon to meet an ailing Giovanni for the first time.

Orphaned, they had been taken in by his grandfather after Nate's father, Benito, and his wife, Anna, had been killed in an alcohol- and drug-fueled car crash. A tragedy to be sure but all Nate could remember was the isolation and bitterness his hardened, eighteen-year-old self had felt at the charmed life his half siblings had led while he and his mother had fought to survive.

The family he'd never been privy to as Benito Di Sione's illegitimate child.

Which was ancient history, Nate told himself as he stepped out onto the veranda with its incomparable views of the sparkling gray-blue sweep of Long Island Sound. He had obliterated that iteration of himself and replaced it with a success story that no one could ignore—not even the aristocrats who loved to snub him.

His grandfather sat in a wooden, high-backed chair, bathed in the dying light of the sun. He turned with that sixth sense of his as Nate approached, a slow smile spreading across his olive-skinned face.

"Nathaniel. I was beginning to think Manhattan had eaten you up whole."

Nate walked around the chair and stood in front of

the man who had come to mean so much to him. A lump formed in his throat at how small, how fragile, his once vital grandfather looked, even more wasted away than their last meeting. And now he knew why.

Giovanni stood and drew him into an embrace. The cancer, his treatments, had robbed his olive skin of its robust glow, turning it a sallow hue. His shoulders felt like skin and bone as Nate closed his fingers around them, his throat thickening with emotion. Despite the very mixed, complex feelings he held toward the Di Sione family, Giovanni had been the self-made, ultra-successful, honorable man Nate had modeled himself after in the wake of his father's failings. In those formative years, when his life could have gone either way with the anger consuming him, his grandfather had been the difference. Had shown him the man he could be.

He drew back, his gaze moving over his grandfather's ravaged face. "Is there nothing that can be done? Are the doctors sure another transplant won't help?"

Giovanni nodded and squeezed his shoulder. "They only did the transplant the first time because of my name and health, you know that. It's my time, Nathaniel. I've had more of a life than many could ever dream of having. I'm at peace with it."

His grandfather sat down and waved him into a chair. Nate took the one opposite him, declining the offer of refreshments from a maid who appeared in the doorway. "I have plans to review when I get back to Manhattan."

Giovanni told the maid to bring Nate a beer. "You work too much," he admonished. "Life is for the living, Nathaniel. Who is going to keep you company the day you have made so many billions you can't hope to spend it all?"

He had already reached that point. For him work, success, was biological, elemental, spurred by a survival instinct that would never rest as long as there was a deal to be made, another building block to be put into place.

"You know I'm not the type to settle down."

"I wasn't talking about the lack of a permanent woman in your life," his grandfather came back wryly, "although that, too, could use some work. I'm talking about you being a workaholic. About you never getting off that jet of yours long enough to breathe fresh air, to register what *season* it is. You're so caught up in making money you're missing the true meaning of life."

Nate lifted a brow. "Which *is*?"

"Family. Roots." His grandfather frowned. "Your nomadic ways, your inability to put a stake in the ground, it won't fulfill you in the long run. I hope you will realize that before it's too late."

"I'm only thirty-five," Nate pointed out. "And *you* are as much of a workaholic, Giovanni. It's our dominant trait. We don't choose it. It chooses us."

"I seem to be gaining some perspective given my current situation." His grandfather's eyes darkened. "That discipline becomes our vice, Nathaniel, when taken to extreme. I failed your father and, by virtue of that, you, by spending every waking moment building Di Sione Shipping."

Nate scowled. "He failed *himself.* He needed to own his vices but he never could."

"There is truth in that." Giovanni pinned his gaze on him. "I know you have your demons. I have them, too. Ones that have haunted me every day of my life. But for you, it's not too late. You have your whole life ahead of you. You have brothers and sisters who care about you, who want to be closer to you, yet you push them away. You want nothing to do with them."

His jaw hardened. "I flew in for Natalia's art exhibition."

"Because you have a soft spot for her." His grandfather shook his head. "Family should be the rock in your life. What sustains you when the storms of life take over."

The suspicious glitter in his grandfather's eyes, the bittersweet note in his voice, made Nate wonder, not for the first time, about the secrets Giovanni had kept from his grandchildren. Why he had left Italy and come to America with only the clothes on his back, never to have contact with his family again.

"We've had this discussion," he told his grandfather, his response coming out rougher than he'd intended. "I have made my peace with my siblings. That has to be enough."

Giovanni lifted a brow. "Is it?"

Nate expelled a breath. Sank into a silence that said this particular conversation was over.

Giovanni sat back in his chair and rested his gaze on the sun, burning its way into the horizon. "I need you to do me a favor. There is a ring that means a great deal to me I would like you to track down. I sold it to a collector years ago when I first came to America. I have no idea where it is or who possesses it. I only have a description I can give you."

Nate was not surprised by the request. Natalia had mentioned at the gallery all of the Di Sione grandchildren except Alex had been sent on quests around the world to find similar treasures for Giovanni. The trinkets that his grandfather called his Lost Mistresses in the childhood tales he had told his grandchildren were, in fact, real entities his siblings had begun to recover: various pieces of precious jewelry, a Fabergé box and the book of poetry Natalia had found for him in Greece along with a husband in Angelos. What the grandchildren couldn't figure out was the significance of the pieces to their grandfather.

Nate nodded. "Consider it done. What do these pieces mean to you, if you don't mind me asking?"

His grandfather's gaze turned wistful. "I hope someday to be able to tell you that. But first, I need to see them again. The ring is very special to me. I must have it back."

"And you will send Alex on the last task," Nate speculated.

"Yes."

His relationship, or the lack of one, he had with his oldest half brother who ran Di Sione Shipping was volatile and complex. Giovanni had made Alex work his way up the ranks to CEO, starting out at the very bottom loading goods at the shipyards, while in contrast, he had appointed Nate to a desk job straight out of the university education he had provided his grandson—compensation, Nate figured, for his having had so little growing up.

But what ran far deeper than this preferential treatment of Nate at Di Sione Shipping, Nate suspected, was that Alex blamed *him* for his parents' death. The night Nate's mother, his father's mistress, had shown up on Benito Di Sione's doorstep, ten-year-old Nate in tow, begging for financial support, had been the night his father had wrapped his car around a tree and killed himself and his wife. There had been a violent argument between the adults prior to the crash, perhaps the precursor to his father's reckless performance behind the wheel.

"Nathaniel?"

Nate shook his head to clear it of things that could never and would never change. "I'll begin the search right away. Is there anything else I can do?"

"Know your brothers and sisters," his grandfather said. "Then I will die a happy man."

An image of Alex's young face in the window that night Nate and his mother had stood on his father's porch begging for assistance filled his head. The confusion written across his brother's face...

Only Alex had known of Nate's existence in the years that had followed, yet he had never once revealed his secret—not until Giovanni had fallen ill. If Nate wondered why, when surely the revelation would have changed his own life irrevocably, when sometimes the question burned a hole right through the center of him, the two brothers had never discussed it.

And really, he thought, shaking his head and bringing himself back to the present, what was the point? Nothing could ever alter the circumstances of that night. What fate had thrown at all of them… Some things were just better off left alone.

Nate put finding Giovanni's ring at the top of his priority list. He gave the description to the private investigator he used to research the mega-million-dollar deals he made on a daily basis and received a response back within forty-eight hours. The ring had been purchased at auction by a Sicilian family decades ago and was, apparently, not for sale.

A patently incorrect term in Nate's book. *Everything* and *everyone* on the planet were for sale if the price tag was high enough. He simply had to come up with a number at which the family would find his offer too sweet to resist.

Concluding his business in New York, he had dinner with his mother, who complained per usual that he was never home, neglected to mention he was doing an errand for Giovanni because the Di Siones were always a sore spot for her, then flew to Palermo on Wednesday. Not known for wasting an opportunity, he checked into the six-star Hotel Giarruso he had been eyeing for acquisition and scheduled a meeting with the consortium who owned it for later that day.

His first order of business after he'd been welcomed into the luxury two-level suite with a personal check-in was to make himself human again. He stepped under a bruisingly hot shower in the palatial marble bathroom on the upper level and closed his eyes, letting the punishing spray beat down on him. No matter how luxurious the jet, how smooth the ride, he never slept on planes. His PA, Josephine, liked to call it the control freak in him, but the truth was he always slept with one eye open, a habit he'd developed while living in a series of sketchy Bronx apartments he and his mother had rented where bad things could and did happen on a regular basis.

Installing his mother in a luxury apartment with 24/7 security and ensuring she never had to work again should have provided him with some level of peace. Instead, his wary nature persisted. When you'd run errands for a neighborhood enforcer for a couple of years in your misguided youth before your mother straightened you out, you knew danger lurked everywhere, particularly for someone with his money and reputation. A smart man kept his eyes open.

His humanity suitably revived, he stepped out of the shower, sluiced the water from his face and grabbed a towel to dry off. Intent on answering a few urgent emails before a catnap and his meeting, he headed down to the lounge. His brain busy running the numbers the lawyers had given him for the hotel's value, he didn't notice the chambermaid bent over the cherrywood bar until he'd taken a couple of steps into the room.

His first impression was that she had the sweetest behind he'd ever seen. Round, firm, shapely buttocks stretched the material of her pewter-colored uniform tight across her hips. Spectacular legs completed the picture. His imagination effortlessly supplemented the rest of the tempting scenario: her face and remaining assets would be equally as luscious.

But what the hell was she doing in his suite?

"Would you mind," he requested deliberately, taking the final two steps into the lounge, "telling me what you are doing here when I left explicit instructions with the butler not to be disturbed?"

She straightened and turned, all in one wary slow-motion move. His gaze slid over her. Her waist in the dress, which was stylish for a chambermaid, was tiny, cinched in just above those delectable hips. Her ample cleavage strained the buttons of the modest, short-sleeved style, as if she was too abundant to be contained in it. Her glossy dark brown hair was caught up in a tight ponytail, her cheekbones high and defined under the most stunning pair of espresso-brown eyes he'd ever seen.

He'd been wrong in his estimation. She wasn't just temptingly attractive—she was one of the most beautiful women he'd ever laid eyes on. Exotic in that olive-skinned, perfectly curved Sicilian sense of the word.

His body tightened as biology demanded in the face of such perfection. He imagined one sultry look from those eyes and most men would be on their knees.

Except right now, he noted, those eyes were aimed at him in a wary perusal, tracing their way down to where the towel was slung around his hips. They widened, darkened into giant espresso orbs. His towel had worked its way lower during his trip down the stairs, sitting now on his hip bones. He was giving her an eyeful. A gentleman would remedy that. But he had never been, nor would he ever be, a gentleman.

This was a six-star hotel he was considering purchasing. He had told his private butler he was not to be disturbed. He wasn't letting it go.

He lifted an eyebrow. "So?"

Dio mio, but he was beautiful. Mina dragged her gaze up to the American's face, her teeth sinking into her bottom lip. He was all defined, perfectly symmetrical muscle, as ideally proportioned as the models in the pictures their teachers had shown them in the anatomy lessons they'd given them in finishing school to prepare the girls to *interact*, as they'd called it, with the opposite sex. As if her classmates hadn't known what the internet was. As if some of them hadn't had their own personal anatomy lesson already...

His dark, brooding gaze slid over her, sending a pulse up her spine. If she had looked up the meaning of *intenso* in the dictionary, his picture would have been right there beside it. Although the glare he wore suggested he had limited patience to go with the definition.

"The butler informed me you were at a meeting." She lifted her chin, pasting a composed look on her face while she searched desperately for the confidence she'd been taught to effortlessly exude. "I knocked before I came in, Signor Brunswick."

"My meeting is this afternoon." His gaze sharpened as it pinned her to the spot. "Isn't that the point of a six-star hotel? To be *six* steps ahead of my schedule, anticipating my every wish?"

Mina's brain went straight to the bedroom on the second level and what this arrogant man would demand of a woman in bed. Her nonexistent experience deferred to her imagination to fill in the blanks. She bet it would be worth every second of her enforced capitulation.

Heat flooded her cheeks. Her fingers tightened around the bar of chocolate she held. His gaze flickered, narrowed, as if he'd read her thoughts down to her final, helpless surrender.

She shifted her weight to both feet, her stomach tying itself in knots. *What was she thinking?* She was *engaged.* And furthermore, she didn't have naughty thoughts like this.

She cleared her throat and held up the chocolate bar. "It *is* my job to anticipate your every need. I was stocking the bar with our fine Sicilian hazelnut chocolate."

The beautiful American strode toward her and took the chocolate out of her hand. A whiff of citrus mixed with spice filled her head. She breathed in deeply as she drank him in. He was even more devastating close up, his thick dark hair spiky and wet from the shower, designer stubble covering the square set of his jaw.

"We make it our policy to know everything about our guests based on past visits," she sputtered nervously. "I brought hazelnut and brazil nut."

He crossed his corded, very fine arms. "Mistake number one...*Lina*," he said, peering at her name tag, which did not use her real name but the name she'd given her manager when she'd taken the job. "I prefer milk chocolate."

"Oh." That threw her for a loop. They were never *wrong* here at Hotel Giarruso. *Ever.* "Well…" she stumbled. "*Sì.* We must have made a mistake. It happens very rarely. I'll fix it."

"What else?" he asked.

"*Scusi?*"

"What else do you know about me, then?"

Other than the fact that he was known to fraternize with tall, beautiful blondes and that she was not to bat an eye if she came across one in his room who was not registered here, despite their strict security policy?

The heat in her cheeks deepened. His gaze narrowed. She desperately filed through the intelligence she'd been given. "We know that you tend to forget to pack the charger for your laptop. I have brought you a universal one."

He walked over to the coffee table. The towel slipped further, giving her an eyeful of chiseled hip bone. *Maledizione.* She needed to get out of here.

He picked up a cord, a charging pack attached. "Not so much of a perk for me this visit."

Her nails dug into her palms as her even-keeled disposition started to slip. *He was something else.* She nodded toward the bar. "We have stocked your favorite single-malt Scotch."

"Predictable."

Her blood started to boil. Being inquisitioned by an arrogant male in a towel that might fall off at any moment was above and beyond the call of duty. *Way* above her pay grade.

She squared her shoulders. "I understand all of this

might not be *revolutionary*, Signor Brunswick, but it's what is expected of us. To surround you with the comforts of home. Although I do agree, we could do better."

Curiosity flashed in those beautiful dark eyes. "Such as?" he purred. "I am all ears."

She took a step back. An amused glitter filled his eyes as he tracked the movement. "I would go beyond cataloging a guest's preferences and start *anticipating* them. For instance, *you* are known to be a morning runner. If it were me arranging things, I would have had a list of suitable routes through some of Palermo's most beautiful neighborhoods sitting on your coffee table for you to follow. Another route to spend much of your run in our most beautiful park. Perhaps one to visit our many famous monuments."

The cynical twist to his mouth smoothed out. "What else?"

"You are a fan of a particular Pinot Noir from the Mount Etna region. I would stock that in your room as we have done so, but I would also include another lesser-known wine from what we Sicilians think is the best vineyard in that region—a wine you cannot purchase in the US."

A gleam of approval fired his eyes. "One more."

She chewed on her lip, her confidence returning. "You are known to appreciate the opera if you are accompanied on a trip with a…*compagno*. I would anticipate an outing for you. Secure tickets at the opera and a gown for the lady, colors suitable for a blonde, of course, as that seems to be your preference."

A smile tugged at his mouth, the dimple that cleaved

his cheek transforming him from arrogant to utterly breathtaking. "And you were on such a roll there with your intriguing ideas, Lina. Until you got to the preference for blondes…"

His gaze blazed a deliberate trail over her high ponytail, down over her face to the slightly strained buttons of her dress she'd been cursing since day one of this job. The pure male appreciation in his eyes made her pulse pound.

"It just so happens my last few *compagnos* have been blonde, but in actual fact, I prefer exotic-looking brunettes."

She forgot to breathe, her head spinning from a lack of oxygen. His stark appraisal was most certainly improper. Most definitely had a message attached to it. She knew she should look away, but the heat coursing through her was like nothing she'd ever felt before. It was like her skin was on fire, like he knew exactly what was under her dress and he wanted his hands all over it.

She took a step back and yanked in a deep breath. *Regained her senses.* "Perhaps," she suggested, lifting her gaze to his, "I can have a bottle of the Pinot Noir delivered to your room?"

His long, dark lashes swept down in a heavy-lidded look. "Will you deliver it personally?"

She gasped. Took another step back. "I'm afraid that won't be possible. I'm off duty in an hour. I have a *date* tonight."

He raised an eyebrow. "Undoubtedly."

The towel slipped another inch. She made a garbled sound at the back of her throat, shoved the other two bars of chocolate in her apron on the table and fled, her muttered, *"Buonanotte..."* followed by his low laughter.

"Enjoy your date, Lina. Don't do anything I wouldn't do."

She thought that since this was Signor Brunswick and his improper towel they were talking about, that might give her a great deal of latitude.

Nate watched the chambermaid go, amusement coursing through him. He didn't remember the last time he'd enjoyed himself so much. Yes, it had been a bit cruel to put the delectable Lina through that, but he was meeting with the owners of this hotel in a few hours and a hotel was only as good as its service. He'd wanted to know what kind of people the Giarruso employed, and Lina had potential.

She clearly had brains to go with her beauty. And not just brains, but a keen understanding of the clientele she served and what could enhance their experience. Which had, in the end, made up for the breach in his privacy and his personal butler's mistake.

His chambermaid's ideas had given him food for thought. Certainly society was moving toward personalization in every industry and the products that were being developed reflected that. To offer his clients things they hadn't even asked for but might appreciate complemented some of the ideas he was already working on. It wouldn't work for every client—some would find it an intrusion. But for others it could prove to be that particular experience, that unique value add that developed in them an affinity for the brand.

He had loved Lina's examples. They were doable, creative ideas that would certainly impress.

His butler appeared with a bottle of Marc de Grazia's Guardiola Mount Etna red just before his meeting. Grown at the highest elevation of any red grape varietal in all of Europe, it looked intriguing.

He slid the bottle into the fridge, a smile on his lips. He'd be lying if he said he didn't wish his delectable chambermaid were here to share it with him. That he would have enjoyed sampling it on her fantastic body. He knew the instant attraction he'd experienced toward her had been reciprocated by the flare of awareness he'd seen in her dark eyes. But she was taken, unfortunately, at least for tonight.

And perhaps that was for the best. He was here to retrieve Giovanni's ring. To fulfill his obligation to his grandfather as quickly as possible so that Giovanni could enjoy the sentimental memories associated with the bauble as long as his life allowed. Perhaps pick up a Palermo-based luxury hotel while he was at it.

Seducing an innocent-looking brunette wasn't in the plans, as much as his macho core wouldn't mind demonstrating to Lina how utterly lacking her date would ultimately prove compared to a night with him.

A pity, really.

CHAPTER TWO

"WHAT'S THE MATTER, *bella mia*?"

Silvio Marchetti, Mina's fiancé, arched a thick, dark brow at her. "You've been distracted ever since we sat down, and since I know it cannot be my scintillating company that is lacking, you must be worrying about something."

Mina, also known as *Lina* when she was entertaining improper men in towels in luxurious hotel suites, blinked. She'd thought she'd done a good job hiding her distraction from her fiancé, but apparently her expressive face, which had been her downfall in the etiquette classes designed to attract a man just like Silvio, continued to plague her.

"Mi dispiace." She waved a hand in the air. "I've had a busy day."

Silvio's thin lips twisted. "Exhausted ordering your team of wedding planners around? It's a good thing I have a big staff, *cara*. You will have many responsibilities as my wife at Villa Marchetti. You must learn how to multitask."

She was quite adept at multitasking! She'd cleaned a whole floor of hotel suites today in addition to surviving Signor Brunswick's improper inquisition. The latter of which was half of the problem with her distraction tonight. She couldn't get the sizzling connection between her and the beautiful American out of her head.

But Silvio didn't know about any of her extracurricular activities. Her job moonlighting as a chambermaid at the Giarruso to pay off the debt her mother had incurred since her father's death was a secret to everyone but her. It wouldn't do for anyone to know Simona Mastrantino's daughter, engaged to one of Italy's wealthiest men, was cleaning toilets by the hour.

She pinned a smile on her face, the fact that her mother would have a coronary if she knew what her daughter was doing to keep things afloat of secondary importance to her bigger problem—her impending marriage to Silvio, which she could not possibly go through with.

"Maybe I'm having prewedding jitters," she murmured. "It's a big production this wedding. So many people will be there."

Silvio reached for her hand and curled his fingers around it. "All you have to do is look beautiful. The rest will be taken care of."

And then they would consummate their relationship. Her stomach dipped at the terrifying thought. She'd never slept with a man. Hadn't had the opportunity with her mother dragging her from one social event to another husband hunting, advertising her innocence like a detail on a high-end real-estate listing. *Look but don't touch*, her mother's vibe had said. And since Mina had never agreed on any of her mother's choices for a rich husband, her mother had chosen for her.

She studied her fiancé as he poured her more of the terrifically expensive Chianti he'd ordered for them, undoubtedly trying to loosen her up. He was classically, undeniably handsome with his chiseled features and straight Roman nose, but his eyes, which Mina did think were the windows to the soul, were hard and unyielding, dominated by thick dark brows that always seemed to frown. She had never once experienced any chemistry whatsoever when he had touched her, *kissed her*, which was as far as he'd managed with her mother on guard.

And yet this afternoon, she acknowledged with a shiver, all it had taken was one look from the American to send electricity coursing through her from her head to her feet. For her to wonder what it would be like to be taken to bed by him. To *know* it would be as good, as *improper*, as everything else about him.

"Mina?"

"Hmm?"

Silvio narrowed his gaze on her. "I was asking if you would like dessert or some Frangelico and coffee… Keep this up, *cara*, and I *will* start thinking it's my company you are finding tiresome."

The desperation that had been coursing through her veins all day with their wedding looming in just forty-eight hours picked up her pulse, sent her heart hammering in her chest.

"What's bothering me," she blurted out, "is that we

hardly know each other, Silvio. Maybe this has all been a bit fast."

That hard edge in his eyes deepened. "Now I *am* thinking you have cold feet, Mina. What more is there to know? I will provide a luxurious life for you to match the one you're accustomed to. You will entertain me in bed and be a good mother to my children. It's very simple."

She pressed a palm to her flushed cheek. She had let the cat out of the bag; she might as well follow through with it.

"When is my birthday?" she asked quietly.

His mouth flattened, a scary, lethal line. "I will, of course, know that when we're married."

"Am I a morning person or a night owl? Can I swim or would I drown if you tossed me over the side of your yacht?"

"I'm considering it," he growled. "*Enough*, Mina."

She sunk her teeth into her bottom lip. "You asked what was wrong. I'm telling you."

Well, not all of it. If she told him the entire truth— that her mother was marrying her off so she inherited the family heirloom, a precious ring her father had bequeathed to her upon her marriage—he might not be so impressed. Of course, she conceded miserably, it changed nothing, really. She was being sold as a possession to bear Silvio Marchetti's *bambinos*, when all she had ever wanted was to go to business school and follow in her father's footsteps.

Silvio threw his napkin on the table. "I think we should get out of here."

Mina's heart collided with the wall of her chest as her fiancé lifted his hand and signaled the waiter. "Perhaps we should have a liqueur," she suggested. *To give this conversation a chance to cool down before they left supervised company.*

He ignored her. Bill secured and paid, he placed a hand at her elbow, brought her to her feet and walked her out of the restaurant with such haste Mina's head swam. She had consumed more than her usual share of wine with dinner with the nerves plaguing her and now it seemed like a particularly bad idea, given she'd gone and voiced thoughts she never should have.

Her mother was going to kill her. Silvio looked like he wanted to kill her.

She was going to face the consequences.

She sat as far away from Silvio as she could in the car that took them home, his usual driver at the helm. Her fiancé sat stone-faced beside her, not uttering a word as they drove through the streets of Palermo to the posh, aristocratic neighborhood of Montepellegrino where she and her mother lived. If it was possible for a man to be utterly furious without showing any outward sign of it, her fiancé had mastered it. His anger emanated from him like a red cloud.

When the car pulled up in front of her mother's house, she breathed a sigh of relief. Silvio got out of the car, came around and opened her door. She took his hand, swung her legs out of the car and straightened. "Silvio—"

"Wait here," her fiancé told his driver in a low tone.

"That isn't necessary," she murmured, panicked because her mother was out at the opera. "I think I'm just tired. I'm sure if I—"

Silvio clamped his fingers hard around hers and propelled her toward the villa. She fumbled in her purse for her keys and found them with shaking fingers. Silvio frowned as she pushed the key into the lock. "Where is the staff?"

"It's Manuel's night off." He had been off for over a year, as in permanently off, but she wasn't about to tell Silvio they had no staff because they were penniless.

Silvio loosened his tie as he walked past her into the salon. "Pour me a drink."

She wanted to refuse, wanted desperately for him to leave, because she didn't like the vibe coming off him, but to reject his suggestion would only add fuel to the fire.

Crossing to the bar, she took a glass from the cabinet and poured him a Cognac, her hands trembling as she put the bottle down. Silvio watched her with a hooded gaze as she turned and carried the glass over to him.

She handed him the tumbler, flinching as his fingers brushed hers. His dark gaze turned incendiary. "We are marrying in front of hundreds of people in two days, Mina. What is behind this sudden display of nerves?"

She didn't love him. She didn't even like him. If the truth be known, she was afraid of him.

Dannazione! If only she could sell the ring her father had left her without marrying him. But the condition in her father's will had been unbreakable. She had to be married to get her hands on the ring.

"It's like I said." She lifted her gaze to her fiancé's.

"It seems very fast and I—I wish I knew you better. I would feel more comfortable."

He took a sip of the Cognac. "You did not go on and on about knowing me when your mother sold you off to the highest bidder. You were happy to snare Palermo's most eligible bachelor. So don't cry foul now, Mina. We will come to know each other."

She lowered her gaze. He was right. It had been as much a business deal as if her mother had forked over an old-fashioned dowry for her except she had nothing and she was being traded for her looks and childbearing ability. Which, she thought hysterically, she didn't even know if she had.

The thud of her fiancé's glass hitting the coffee table brought her head up. "Perhaps you are nervous about *us*," he suggested. "You've been playing the ice queen so long we haven't had a chance to get properly acquainted." His eyes glittered as he wrapped his fingers around her wrist and drew her to him. "Since we are very nearly married, I suggest we take some time to do that now."

Her heart thumped in her chest. "My mother—"

"—is at the opera." He brought his mouth down on hers. "You mentioned that earlier."

He kissed her then, a hard, demanding press of his mouth that was about punishment, not pleasure. Her heart galloped faster at the secure hold he had on her wrist. He was tall and big and she could never get away unless he chose to let her.

He didn't. His mouth continued to punish her, the hand he had on her waist moving down to cup her buttocks through the thin silk of her dress. He pulled her against him in an intimate hold she had never experienced before, his aroused body pressing against hers. It set off alarm bells in her head. "Silvio," she gasped, twisting away from his mouth. "Not like this…"

His face contorted with rage. "It will be *exactly* as I want it, *cara*. *Any* way I want it."

"Silvio—"

He brought the flat of his hand across her cheek so hard her head snapped to the side. Her ears rang with the force of it, her head spinning as a white-hot throb spread across her cheek.

"Refuse me again," he bit out, "and you will discover the depths my anger can sink to. I will not hear one more word of your silly jitters, Mina. Nor will I tolerate you repeating any of them to *anyone*. You are going to be my wife in two days. Our union is the talk of this city. Get yourself together."

The sound of keys in the door brought her head around. Her mother walked in, her gaze flicking from Mina to Silvio, then back again, eyes widening at the mark on Mina's face. "I thought that was your car, Silvio."

Silvio released her and stepped back. Sparing her mother a brief nod, he stalked past her to the door. "My driver will pick you up for the rehearsal dinner at six thirty tomorrow."

The door slammed. Mina's mother unwound her scarf from around her neck and walked slowly toward her, her gaze wary. "What was that?"

The moment she'd found out her fiancé was a vio-

lent man. Mina sank down on the sofa and buried her face in her hands.

"I can't marry him."

Her mother sat down beside her. "Let me see your face."

She lifted her head, utterly sure when her mother saw the welt she would agree she couldn't marry Silvio. Her mother sighed, went to the bar for ice, wrapped some in a towel and came back to sit down beside her, pressing it to her cheek. "What Sicilian man doesn't have a temper?"

Mina froze, disbelief plummeting through her, followed by a deep rage that sent blood pumping to every inch of her skin. "Did Father ever hit *you*?"

Her mother's lips pursed. "Your father was a different kind of man."

Yes, he had been. Honorable and loving. He would no more have lifted a hand to his wife or daughter than he would have kicked a dog on a street corner, which, she was sure, Silvio Marchetti would do. She was also sure from what had just happened, her fiancé's behavior would escalate when she was under his roof as his wife.

"I won't do it. We can find someone else."

Her mother shook her head, a resigned look on her face. "You have rejected every choice I've made for over a year now, Mina. You are marrying in front of half of Palermo in two days. Life is not all sunshine and rainbows. Sacrifices must be made and we need your sacrifice now. You know that."

Her mother was okay with sacrificing her to a ruthless, violent man?

Dio mio. She'd always known she was heartless, but *this*… What kind of a monster was she?

Her mother's gaze softened. "I suggest you find some peace with this. Men are men. You happen to be marrying a filthy rich one. Let that be your comfort."

CHAPTER THREE

MINA'S WEDDING DAY dawned sunny and crisp, ushering in the first day of fall in true, glorious Palermo fashion.

Bright rays of sunshine stole through the curtains that swayed in her open bedroom windows, a light breeze kissing her shoulders with a jasmine-scented caress. Temperatures were supposed to skyrocket to an unseasonable warmth as the afternoon went on, making it the perfect day for the lavish outdoor reception she and Silvio would host at Villa Marchetti.

Soon it would be time to slip on the stunning dress hanging in her wardrobe and make her way by horse and carriage to the elegant Palermo cathedral to wed her wealthy, influential groom.

A fairy-tale day it should have been. But inside, Mina was filled with dread. She couldn't seem to function, her every muscle and limb numb as the minutes passed, her stomach barely holding down the light breakfast she'd managed to consume. Today she would marry Silvio, a man she didn't love, who had turned out to be a hot-tempered, violent man. Everything she'd suspected he could be and more. And nothing she had said or done to convince her mother she couldn't do it had worked.

She stared in the mirror as her mother layered thick concealer over the bruise Silvio had left on her cheek, not a hint of emotion on Simona Mastrantino's face to indicate she felt any degree of empathy for her daughter.

"Makeup is a woman's magic." Her mother swept another layer of the thick concealer over her cheek. "No one will see the bruise. But you must remember to tuck this in your purse for touch-ups later with the photographs."

Mina absorbed this latest piece of advice from her mother dazedly, wondering if she could truly be this heartless. There was no question their relationship had always been strained, distant. Simona Mastrantino had made it clear from the very beginning she had no interest in being a mother—she had done it only to keep her husband happy. Off to the nannies Mina had gone while her mother lived a socialite's glamorous life as the wife of the CEO of one of Italy's most successful companies.

Mina had accepted this state of affairs with the innocent obliviousness of a child who knew no different. That Camilla, her nanny, and her beloved *papà* were her source of love and affection, her mother a beautiful, foreign creature who was to be awed from afar, like one of her beautiful dolls, had been her reality.

Her chest throbbed at the memory of her *papà*. He had always come to her first when he'd gotten home, swung her up in his arms and called her his *piccolo tesoro*, his little treasure, as he'd carried her off to bed to read. The bond between father and daughter had been inviolate, her *papà* lavishing upon her the attention her mother had not.

Until the day she'd come home from school to find her *nonna*, Consolata, at the house, and her father dead of a massive heart attack. Mina had clung to her *nonna*, her eight-year-old face a river of tears as she'd begged her to take her to see her father, perhaps instinctively knowing her last grounding force had been taken away. But her *nonna* had refused all of Mina's hysterical demands, telling her a hospital was no place for a child.

The dust had barely settled on her father's grave when her mother had sold the family business and packed a grieving Mina off to boarding then finishing school. Ripped away from everything she knew, without the unconditional love of her father or Camilla, Mina had floundered, filled with confusion and guilt. What was it about her that caused her mother to reject her so completely? It had been her good schoolfriend Celia and her mother, Juliana, who had become a surrogate mother to Mina, who had saved her from the shadows of those miserable years.

Her mother had only recognized Mina's importance when she'd come of age, an attractive bauble to dangle before Palermo's most eligible bachelors to solve their financial problems. Then it had been a relentless pursuit to find her a rich husband to marry, not the bonding Mina had craved.

A lump formed in her throat. "Please don't ask me

to do this," she begged her mother through frozen lips, repeating the appeal she'd already made twice today. "We can find someone else, *Mamma*."

Her mother's gaze hardened with impatience. "We've been through this, Mina. You had your chance to pick someone else. You chose no one. I chose Silvio. Stop being so childish and selfish. You are doing your duty to this family. Marry Silvio, sell the ring and all our problems will be solved."

All her mother's problems would be solved. *Hers would just be beginning.* She closed her eyes. This was not how it was supposed to go. Today *was* supposed to be sunshine and rainbows. Her father was supposed to be walking her down that aisle toward a man as besotted with her as her father had been with her mother.

After she'd made a life for herself. After she'd followed in her father's brilliant business footsteps. She may not have Felicia Chocolate left—the family chocolatier her mother had sold—but her time spent in France studying and attaining top grades, learning of the vast and varied world out there, had taught her she could never limit herself to the traditional role of a woman in Sicily. She wanted more, so much more, for herself.

But all of that would be for naught if she married Silvio today. Her fingers curled around the arms of the chair, her knuckles gleaming white. She would spend her days pregnant with his *bambinos*, relegated to an artifact in his beautiful, cold, austere home.

The wedding planner's assistant swept back into the room, Mina's dress draped over her arm, having given mother and daughter a discreet few minutes to cover Silvio's damage. "Are we ready for the dress?"

Her mother straightened and nodded. The wedding planner gave Mina a once-over. "Excellent. You look beautiful."

Mina stood as the wedding planner moved to her side to help her on with the fairy-tale dress, one worthy of Silvio Marchetti's wife. She lifted her arms as the assistant dropped the dress over her head and settled it down around her hips in a whisper of silk and lace. She obediently pulled in a breath as the dress was done up, hugging every curve of her body with its slim, tulip shape. Except she didn't need to expend the effort as the dress did up easily. Too easily. She'd lost weight the last few weeks of fretting.

The wedding planner tutted about this latest wrinkle, producing pins to close the gap below the low, dipping back of the dress. Mina surveyed herself in the mirror, a tumult of emotion swirling through her. She looked impeccable. The dress was perfect, her hair an elegant chignon with tiny, white flowers woven through it, her face a subtle, painted masterpiece.

And it was all wrong. She could not do this. She could not.

Silver stilettos and the diamond choker and drop earrings Silvio had given her as a wedding gift completed her irreproachable appearance. And then it was time to go. She descended the wide circular staircase to the main level of the villa, the wedding planner managing her modest train behind her.

She had not even a bridesmaid to commiserate with.

Celia was managing a big product launch in Paris and hadn't been able to make it, which meant the bridesmaids were all Silvio's—strangers to her.

She waited in the salon for the horse and carriage that would transport her to the church. Her mother and the planner would ride on ahead in the limousine Silvio had sent for them to ensure everything was ready for her arrival.

A cloud of perfume preceding her, her mother brushed a kiss against her cheek. "Brighten up, Mina. You will have everything after this."

Except what she really wanted. Her freedom. A man who actually loved her.

The door closed behind her mother in a waft of jasmine and she was alone. Alone in the beautiful dress that flowed around her, the diamond choker growing tighter around her throat with every second that passed.

Her breathing grew shallow, her palms sweaty. She was out of time. Out of options.

The elegant old Mastrantino villa was located in the aristocratic neighborhood of Montepellegrino, with its sweeping views of Palermo, the surrounding mountains and the Tyrrhenian Sea.

As much as Nate appreciated the spectacular view, he was more interested in speaking with the Mastrantinos, acquiring Giovanni's ring and wrapping up his business in Sicily so he could complete stops in Capri, Hong Kong and the Maldives before heading home to hand the ring over to his grandfather.

He had elected not to pursue the Giarruso at this point

in time, as it wasn't quite the unique opportunity he'd been searching for to enhance his portfolio—delectable smart chambermaids aside.

The handsome, elegantly stuccoed Mastrantino villa looked as quiet as it had the night before when he'd come seeking the ring only to find no one home. Hoping his luck was better today, Nate asked his driver to wait at the front entrance, strode up the wide set of steps to the front entrance and rang the bell.

When no one answered, he rang again, impatience thrumming through his veins. *Why were there no staff members answering the door?* Were the Mastrantinos out of town? He scowled. That would put a major kink in his plans.

He was about to ring a third time when the door opened and he was faced with a vision in white. A dark-haired vision in white. A wedding dress to be exact, floating around the woman's incredible figure. He lifted his gaze to her beautiful face and shock flooded through him. *Lina. Here?*

"I thought you were my horse and carriage," she breathed, hiking up the train of her dress.

He looked down at her silver, high heel–clad dainty feet, then back at the luxury sedan his driver had parked at the curb, wondering dazedly if he'd been transported into some bizarre real-life Cinderella re-enactment. "No," he replied slowly, looking back at Lina, "I most definitely came on four wheels."

She blinked. "Signor Brunswick. What *are* you doing here?"

He noticed then the tears that streaked her perfect

makeup, the vulnerable tilt to her chin, the quiver to her mouth, and *damn* if it didn't tear him up inside.

He dragged his gaze back up to hers. "I am looking for the Mastrantinos. Do you live here?"

Her beautiful mouth quivered some more. He ran a hand through his hair. Cursed. Comforting emotional women was not his forte.

She pressed her lips together. "Now is not a very good time."

No kidding. She was apparently getting married today. Not just taken, but marrying someone.

Why was she crying on her wedding day? He was no expert but he had been led to believe it was every woman's dream.

He swallowed. "I am looking for Simona or Mina Mastrantino. They own a ring I would like to purchase. But since this is clearly *not* a good time, as you say, I can come ba—"

"What ring?" Her dark gaze fixed on his.

"The Fountain Ring with the sapphire in it."

Her eyes widened. "How do you know about that ring?"

"My private investigator tracked it down for me. I want to purchase it."

"Why?"

"It has…sentimental value for someone close to me."

A woman walking down the avenue gave them a curious look. Lina stepped back and motioned for him to come in. He stepped in and she shut the door behind him.

"I am…Mina Mastrantino," she said haltingly, digging her teeth into her bottom lip in that trademark nervous tic of hers. "I—I don't use my real name when I work. But you can't—I mean—please keep that between us."

Who was he going to tell? And—*what? Lina was Mina?* Why in God's name was she working as a chambermaid?

Lina, or rather *Mina*, gestured to a room to the left. "Please come in. Sit down."

He walked past her into the richly appointed, slightly outdated salon which had clearly once been the showpiece of the villa with its hand-carved fireplaces, crystal chandeliers and elegant arches. Mina followed and indicated a chair for Nate while she perched on a sofa. He sat down, his gaze moving over the distraught bride's face.

Her eyes were full of turmoil as she lifted them to his. "I would love to sell you the ring, Signor Brunswick, but unfortunately, I cannot."

"Nate," he corrected. She had seen him in a towel, after all. "And why not?"

"It's a family heirloom. My father bequeathed it to me upon my marriage."

He looked pointedly at her expensive wedding dress. "Which is happening today…"

"Yes." Her lips started to quiver again, a tear escaping those dark-as-night eyes.

His blood pressure shot through the roof. *Dear Lord, he didn't need this right now. He really didn't.*

"Mina." He moved across the room to sit beside her on the sofa, likely not the smartest move given the chemistry between them, but he couldn't help himself as he lifted a hand to her delicate jaw to turn her face to him. Her dark lashes were soaked with tears that ran down her cheek like sparkling crystals. Her sultry mouth was vulnerable and bare of color. Undeniably enticing. But it was the dark shadow on her cheek the sunlight pouring in through the windows revealed that caught his attention. Turned his blood to ice.

He knew it was none of his business, knew he should walk out the door right now and come back tomorrow, but he couldn't seem to move. He was a smart man. He could put two and two together and he did not like what he saw.

"Your fiancé," he said quietly, dangerously, "gave you that bruise on your cheek?"

Her fingers flew up to cover it. "Oh, no, I—"

"Mina…"

She stared at him, dropped her head into her hands and sobbed.

Dammit all. Nate wrapped his arm around her and pulled her onto his lap, cradling her against his chest. She stiffened against him as if ready to bolt, then another sob racked her petite body and she melted into him, her tears soaking his shirt. Shredding his self-possession.

He held her as she cried, ruthlessly commanding his all too aware body that the soft curves that fit so perfectly against him were utterly off-limits. His hand stroked her silky hair, nudging some curly tendrils free from the perfect knot as her sobs dissolved into sniffles, but he didn't care. She was trembling like a leaf.

"Tell me," he ordered, "what is going on here."

She shook her head. "Silvio—my fiancé—he's a very powerful man. He would kill me if I said anything."

He lifted her chin with his fingers. "Funny thing about that, Mina, but I'm a powerful man, too, and I don't hit my women. Silvio *who*?"

She squeezed her eyes shut. "Silvio Marchetti. He owns half of Sicily. You really don't want to get mixed up with him."

He would like to get *very* mixed up with Silvio Marchetti right now. *Violently, aggressively* mixed up with Silvio Marchetti. Unfortunately, he wasn't here for him to inflict the desired punishment.

"Why are you marrying a monster?"

Her dark eyes shone like polished ebony. "He is my mother's choice. It's been…arranged."

He gave her an incredulous look. "That still happens?"

"Here it does."

"Does your mother know he hits you?"

Her chin wobbled.

Hell. "Tell her you won't."

"I have. I—we need this match."

"Why?" She could hardly *need* it.

Mina shook her head. "It doesn't matter. Everyone is at the church already. I am marrying Silvio in front of half of Palermo in—" she looked at her watch "—less than an hour."

"Call it off," he grated. "You can't possibly marry him, Mina. *Look* at you."

She pushed a hand against his chest to get up. He held her firm. "*Why* are you doing this?"

"Because we need the money," she bit out. "I need to marry to get the ring so I can sell it and pay off our debts. My mother and I are *bankrupt*. That's why I was working at the hotel."

So she was going to marry a violent man to make that happen?

He let her go. Watched as she stood and paced the room, the train of her dress following behind her. "Why not marry someone of your own choosing, then?"

"I told you already." She stopped and jammed her hands on her hips. "My mother arranged the match. Silvio was the last of a dozen candidates she put forward. I am out of choices."

"Why did you reject the others?"

"Because I didn't love them."

Oh, boy. She was one of *those.* He hated to burst Ms. Mastrantino's bubble at this particular dire moment in time but… "Love is a myth, Mina." He gave her a hard look. "Find a man you're comfortable with, who treats you right, and marry him."

"It's too late for that." Her gaze swung to the window, a frantic, trapped look in her eyes. "The carriage will be here any minute."

He studied the tension in every muscle of her slim body. The panicked aura that wove itself around her. She was truly terrified. And why not? She was about to marry an abusive man in minutes.

In that moment, he realized he could not leave Mina here to suffer that fate. It was *insane, ludicrous.* He had certainly never pegged himself as anyone's Prince Charming, but he was not walking away and abandoning this vulnerable woman to a violent man. It went against every code of honor his mother had drilled into him.

He stood up and joined her at the window. She turned to look at him, a glazed, resigned expression on her face. "What would you do if you had a choice?" he asked. "If you could marry someone other than Silvio and sell the ring?"

"I would pay off our debts," she said quietly, "walk away and start a new life for myself."

"Silvio will be furious," he said. "To have his bride jilt him at the altar in front of the whole city. You would have to leave town. And quickly."

She stared at him, wide-eyed. "I was merely speaking in 'what ifs.' Of course I would never do it. It's far too late now."

He held her gaze. "Someone I care about very deeply wants that ring back. It was once his—years ago he had to sell it to survive. *You* need to get out of this situation. There is no way you can marry Silvio. So I'm proposing a business solution. Marry me, sell me the ring and I will fly you out of here tonight on my jet. We'll get the marriage annulled immediately after the deal is done. We both get what we need."

She gaped at him. "That is…*crazy.* I—I don't even know you. Silvio will—" she waved a hand at him, the multicarat ring she had not been wearing while cleaning blinding in the light "—lose his mind."

"You had me vetted at the Giarruso," he reminded

her. "They do full security checks. And you know this isn't going to get any better. If he's hit you once, he'll hit you again. And again. Until you'll think it's normal to greet the day with bruises. *If* he doesn't send you to the hospital with broken bones."

She stared at him mutely.

"My jet is waiting on standby." He kept his gaze on hers, steady and sure. "I'm offering you a way out of this. The decision is yours. If you choose to marry Silvio, I can come back at a mutually agreed upon time and make you an offer for the ring."

Her cheeks drained of color. She pressed her hands to them and shook her head. "I don't know what to do."

"Make a decision,' he advised, casting a deliberate look toward the window. "And fast. When that carriage arrives, you are out of options."

She paced the length of the room. Back and forth. Finally, she stopped in front of him, her small palms curled into fists by her sides. "You are really willing to do this? What about whatever woman is in your life? How is she going to feel about it?"

His mouth lifted. "There is no current woman, and even if there was, she'd know marriage is never in the cards for me. I'm fine with this, Mina. The question is are you?"

Her chin moved up and down.

"Is that a yes?"

"Sì."

"You're sure?" He held her gaze with his. "You have to be sure. There's no turning back."

"I'm sure." Fear filled her eyes. "What if Silvio comes after us?"

"I will deal with him," he said roughly. *God help the man if he got his hands on him.*

He swung into execution mode. "Get your purse and passport. Everything else can wait."

She turned on her heel and walked out of the room, elaborate dress trailing behind her. Nate raked his hair out of his face. This might be the most unique business deal he'd ever made, but it certainly wasn't the most complex. This one was simple. Marry the girl, get the ring and have their union annulled. As far as marriages went, it was the kind he could wrap his head around.

Mina was in shock. She must be, she decided as she sat in the backseat of the luxury car alongside Nate and attempted to contemplate the enormity of what she was doing. At this very minute, she was standing up Silvio Marchetti, one of Sicily's most powerful figureheads, *at the altar* where her mother and her family and everyone they had known for generations were waiting for her to appear.

An image of her fiancé's hard, unyielding face with its cruel edge flickered through her head. The incredulity of her failure to show up spreading across it until that white-hot rage of his set in. He *would* lose his mind. He would take it out on those around him. Her hands, laced together in her lap upon the fine silk of her dress, went ice-cold.

Would he take it out on her mother as the next best thing to her? Would her mother ever forgive her?

Simona Mastrantino might be an unfeeling, ambitious, repressed aristocrat willing to trade on her daughter's fate, but she was all the family Mina had.

Would Silvio send his henchmen after her when he discovered what had happened? Did he *have* henchmen?

Her stomach heaved, a determined swallow all that was keeping her breakfast in her stomach. She was giving up *everything* she knew, agreeing to marry a man she hardly knew, to start a life far away from her home. Where would she go? To Paris where Celia was? Where she could use her French? Or was that too close to danger?

Nate continued to make phone call after phone call on his mobile, barking out orders in that deep authoritative tone of his. Phrases and words flew by in rapid succession. Civil ceremony, marriage license, documentation, *prenup*.

Nate flicked her a glance. "Can you have your solicitor give us the ring today? It would be better for us to leave tonight rather than wait around until the open of business tomorrow morning."

Which might give Silvio a chance to track her down in a murderous rage. She shivered. "I will call him and find out."

A quick conversation with Pasquale Tomei determined they were in luck. He had the ring in his home for safekeeping and could see them late afternoon. Which gave them time to marry first.

They pulled up at the Giarruso minutes later. She kept her head down as Nate put a hand to her back and guided her past curious onlookers through the front doors of the hotel and into the elevators to the penthouse suites. She breathed a sigh of relief as they rode skyward having avoided anyone she knew.

Everything happened in a blur after that. The arrival of the Giarruso butler with the prenuptial agreement Nate's lawyer had sent along with a bouquet of beautiful white flowers for Mina and two simple, elegant gold bands. She kept her back turned as her colleague offered his congratulations to Nate, then left.

The civil registrar who had miraculously been produced to marry them arrived next. It was a testament to the authority of the stranger who was about to become her husband as every detail fell into rapid-fire place, nothing beyond his control.

Then she was standing by Nate's side, her groom-to-be now dressed in a dark, expensive-looking suit rather than the jeans and shirt he'd had on when he'd arrived at her home. *Insanely handsome.*

The registrar began the short, textbook ceremony. Mina recited the words in Italian, Nate in English, words that should have been a sacred affirmation of a love that would last forever conducted in a church with a priest as with the traditions of her own faith.

Nate captured her hand in his as the ceremony came to a close, his dark, fathomless eyes holding hers as he slid the sparkling gold band on her finger. She swallowed hard, took the ring he handed her and slid it onto his elegant, strong hand. A flash of sensual awareness pierced the numbness blanketing her as the heat of his skin bled into hers. Those beautiful hands would be eminently capable of handling a woman.

Devastatingly exciting. Too bad she would never get to find out how exciting.

Her gaze lifted to his, curiosity plastered all over her face. A dark gleam entered his inscrutable gaze, injecting his almost black eyes with a heat that stole her breath.

The registrar indicated Nate could kiss his bride. He lowered his head to hers, his hands resting lightly on her waist to draw her closer. "Just to keep it real," he murmured in her ear.

He pulled back and set his gaze on her lips. Her heart pounded in her chest as he bent his head and claimed her mouth in a whisper-soft kiss, his hard, sensuous lips settling against the pillowy softness of hers with unerring accuracy. For a moment she remained frozen, neither responding nor rejecting. Nate edged her lips further apart with a light pressure that commanded rather than asked. With a helpless sigh, she relaxed against him, sinking into his warmth as his hand came up to cup her jaw, angling her for his consumption.

It was every bit as good as she'd imagined it would be. She grabbed a handful of his shirt to steady herself, knees weak. She'd been kissed before, surely, by a couple of men, but never like this. Never so expertly, so *thoroughly*.

Utterly under his spell, a soft sound escaped her throat. The officiant gave a delicate cough. Nate's hands fell away from her face as he put some distance between them, a flare of something she couldn't read blazing in his eyes. *Disappointment? Desire?*

Her heart, already sorely under duress, beat a jagged rhythm. *What was she doing? Making out with a playboy like Nate Brunswick—her soon-to-be ex-husband?*

Nate turned to thank the registrar, apparently not as gobsmacked by the kiss as she had been. She attempted to gather her composure as he moved with ruthless efficiency to tie up loose ends with the officiant, summoned a bellboy to gather their things and had the car brought around.

When they were ensconced in the back of the sedan again, headed toward the affluent, beachside suburb of Mondello where her solicitor lived, Mina rested her head back against the seat and closed her eyes. Relived that *kiss*. How her knees had literally melted beneath her.

"Are you okay?"

Deep and velvety soft, Nate's sinful voice interrupted her recap.

She opened her eyes. "Why did you do that?"

"Do what?"

"The kiss. That *kiss*."

Amusement darkened his gaze. "That wasn't a kiss, Mina. That was a peck on the mouth to satisfy the registrar's expectations."

She wondered what a real kiss from him would be like. *Unforgettable*, she imagined.

"I will concede," he drawled, his eyes on the hot color flooding her face, "that we have some kind of chemistry, *wife*. Too bad it's a marriage in name only."

She laced her hands together in her lap and glued her eyes to them.

"Surely you've kissed Silvio," he prodded. "Perhaps even bedded him? I looked him up, Mina. He has quite a reputation."

She lifted her chin. "Silvio has always been a gentleman."

His brows lifted.

"Well, until that…*incidente*."

Nate sat back in the seat, arms crossed over his chest after that, watching her with an enigmatic look. Likely glad he was getting rid of her shortly…

They made the reasonably short trip to her solicitor's home quickly in the quiet Sunday traffic.

Pasquale Tomei smiled as he opened the door of his Liberty-style villa. His smile faded as his gaze moved over Mina in her wedding dress and then to Nate. "Where is Silvio?"

"She married me, not him," Nate said matter-of-factly. "True love and all that."

Pasquale's eyes widened. Mina pushed a stray chunk of hair out of her face and straightened her spine. "We are in a bit of a hurry, Pasquale. If you could give us the ring, we can be on our way."

"I'll need to see the paperwork." The solicitor waved them into the house. "There are terms I need to explain."

Terms? Mina frowned as they followed the lawyer down a hallway and into his office. Sitting down beside Nate on the opposite side of the desk, she handed Pasquale their paperwork. He looked it over and handed it back. "This is quite a change in plans. Your mother was very excited about your and Silvio's union."

The color drained from her face. "Mina is free to marry whom she chooses," Nate interceded, a blunt edge to his voice. "So if we could have the ring..."

Pasquale took a box out of the drawer and handed it to Mina. She opened the navy blue velvet jeweler's box and there it was. The Fountain Ring. A stunning square-cut sapphire of the deepest blue surrounded by diamonds set in a platinum band. A beautiful piece to be sure, but it was its extensive history and the mystery that surrounded the ring's origins that made it so valuable.

She closed the box and looked at Pasquale. "What were the terms you spoke of?"

The lawyer set forth a sheaf of papers that had been sitting on his desk, moving to a page he had marked with a colored tab. "There is one condition I must make you aware of. You must remain married for one year for me to grant you full title of the ring."

If there was any color left in her face, it fled now. Nate's jaw dropped open. *"Why?"*

"Mina's father wanted to see her happily married before the ring was made hers."

Mina shook her head. "That condition was never mentioned to me."

"I'm sorry," the lawyer said. "But as you can see, it's there in black and white."

She turned to absorb the silent tension in the man beside her. His usual even expression was firmly in place, but in his eyes she could read fury. *Barely leashed fury.*

He directed a look at the lawyer. "Mina can keep the ring in her possession during this time?"

"Yes."

"Fine." Nate closed his fingers around her shoulder as he stood up, propelling her with him. "We should go."

They thanked the lawyer. Nate hurried her down the steps and into the waiting car, giving the driver a curt instruction to take them to the airport. *To step on it.*

Her stomach dropped. She waited until the privacy screen had come up between them and the driver before she said quietly, "You are worried he will tip off Silvio."

"Or your mother."

Right. That would be just as bad because her mother would go straight to Silvio and... She took a deep breath and forced herself to remain calm. A tense silence stretched between them. "Nate—" she said haltingly. "I didn't know."

He turned his dark, blazing gaze on her. "It's a pretty big detail to not know about, Mina, given your desire to get your hands on the ring and sell it."

She pressed her lips together. "I was never told about this condition. I *swear*, I did not know."

His gaze raked her face. She squared her shoulders under its hard, cold weight. "What are the terms in the document?"

"What do you mean?"

"I mean, do we have to *live together*? Are there any other stipulations attached to the marriage?"

She shook her head. "That's all the document said."

He lapsed into silence. She curled up in her corner

of the seat, blood pounding against her temples. What if he abandoned their agreement? Left her here for Silvio to punish? She had no money, no possessions, *nothing* to get away.

Long moments passed. When she was teetering on the edge of complete and irreversible panic, he turned to her, icy control back in his face. "What was your plan after we left? Where were you intending on having me take you?"

She shook her head, her mouth trembling. "I—I don't have one. I just left my fiancé at the altar, Nate. I—I'm—"

In shock.

"Okay," he said finally after a long moment. "Here's what we're going to do. We're going to get on my jet, we're going to fly to Capri where I have business to attend to, and we will sort this out on the way."

"Capri?"

His mouth tightened. "That's the destination on offer."

She closed her eyes. What choice did she have? Her first course of action had to be to get out of here. Then she could regroup.

The miles flew by and then they were at the airport, an expedited process seeing them quickly through security. The official asked for her passport. Mina handed it to him and smiled when he gave it back. Nate gripped her elbow in a tight hold and started walking her through the doors toward the tarmac. *Fast.*

"Keep your head down," he muttered. "And keep walking."

Her reflexive action, of course, was to turn her head. Two men in dark suits stood arguing with the guards covering the security checkpoint. Her breath caught in her throat.

"*Dio mio.* Nate—"

"Put your head down," he barked, "and walk. He isn't going to touch you. I promise."

She kept walking, her knees threatening to give way beneath her. Nate slid his arm around her waist and propelled her forward. Up the steps to the jet they went, the doors closing behind them. Nate told her to sit down and buckle up, then walked into the cockpit to say something to the pilot.

In minutes they were cleared to leave by the control tower. Mina had never felt so light-headed in all her life as they taxied down the runway and took off, lifting sharply as a gust of wind buoyed them higher.

Dread consumed her. "It was Silvio, wasn't it?" She turned to look at Nate as her stomach rose and fell with the ascending aircraft. "Who sent those men?"

CHAPTER FOUR

NATE SURVEYED MINA'S panicked expression, her fear as she curled her hands around the armrests, knuckles white, overriding the fury he felt at his now excessively complicated life. *The fury he felt toward the abusive man who had just tried to come after her.*

"I suspect so," he said grimly. "I will find out for certain. But there's no need to worry. He can't touch you now."

Her eyes flashed. "What if he sends his men after me? Pasquale could give him all our information."

"Then he will know I am not a man to be messed with. That it's fruitless to come after you."

"You're only one man. You saw the men he sent."

"He won't get past my security detail."

"Security detail?"

"I'm a rich man, Mina. It's a prerequisite."

She sat back in her chair, looking so chalk white he feared she might pass out. When the attendant came around to offer them drinks he asked for two glasses of brandy and put one in front of Mina.

"I don't drink liquor."

"Today you do." He nodded toward the glass. "Drink. It'll help your nerves."

She stared dubiously at the amber liquid. Took a little sip and wrinkled her nose. "I don't like it."

"Keep drinking."

He leaned back against the seat, resting his brandy on his thigh. His temporary wife was now his wife for a year, *a year*, a state of being he had never once contemplated entering into nor wanted. That was *if* he chose to go through with the deal he and Mina had made, a *vastly* different one than he had signed on for.

He took in the stunning, innocent creature who was now his wife. Her disheveled hair, streaked makeup and worry lined face. His cynical side suggested she might have known about the year-long clause in the will, perhaps had seen an opportunity for escape in him that had been sweetened by the idea of a rich husband. But his gut told him that wasn't the case. Mina hadn't even blinked when he'd said the word *prenup*. She'd looked as frozen, as in shock, as he'd been when Pasquale Tomei had unveiled that condition. It could not have been manufactured.

With that stipulation, the key to her escape had been stripped from her, the ability to start a life away from her clearly uncaring mother and abusive ex-fiancé. *He* had been the one walking into the middle of things offering solutions. And now he had a much bigger one to find.

What was he going to do with a wife? With Mina? He couldn't just dump her in Capri and tell her to contact him when she could sell him the ring. Marchetti was too likely to get to her there.

She needed his protection. *He* needed that ring to show Giovanni before he died. To give him a chance to reconnect with the past. Which meant his wife was now his responsibility. For a year.

"When you talked about obtaining your freedom," he said, "what did you envision yourself doing?"

"I speak multiple languages. I thought I would follow in my father's footsteps. Become a business-woman."

"Do you have a business degree?"

"No." She pressed her lips together, her dark gaze dropping away from his. "I went to a finishing school in France."

A *finishing school*. Did those still *exist*? "And your father. What business was he in?"

"He was the CEO of our family chocolate company—Felicia. It was one of the biggest in Europe before my mother sold it to an American conglomerate."

He took a sip of his drink. "Most people who want to get into business today have studied it in school. It's very difficult to find a position without a degree or a diploma."

Her chin rose. "I expect to start out at the bottom. I'd thought maybe I could work as a chambermaid at the Giarruso, then find a higher position."

Admirable if wishful thinking. Unless, of course, a superior was willing to give her a shot in the business as Giovanni had given him.

He thought back to Mina's quick, well-thought-out

answers that day at the Giarruso. She had the natural business instincts he himself had once had. A moldable brain. *Was it time for him to pay it forward? To give her the same chance he had been given?*

He had been eighteen, working the night shift at a food warehouse, when Alex had tracked him down to save Giovanni. Eighteen and angry. His mother had managed to straighten him out after his run-in with the dark side in his midteens, begging him to stop running errands for the neighborhood enforcer before he got himself shot or killed. But she hadn't been able to convince him to go back to school. They needed the money and he couldn't just stand by and watch her work herself into her grave while he studied in a useless English lit class.

He'd taken a job at the warehouse where he'd discovered what hell truly felt like. Eight-hour night shifts in the dank, cavernous space, the fluorescent lights beating into his temples as he broke his back hauling flat after flat of produce into place.

He remembered leaving work one morning a few months after he'd started, the faint light of dawn creeping across the sky. Back killing him, lungs tight, he'd stopped and leaned against the building, wondering if this miserable existence was life. Because if this was what it was, he didn't want it. At least when he'd been working the streets he'd had money in his pocket. He'd had his self-respect. He'd *been* somebody.

For the first time in years, he'd allowed his hatred toward his father loose, driving his fist into the concrete facade of the warehouse, leaving him with two broken fingers and no less bitterness. He hadn't wanted a life like his half siblings' lives—but to be the result of his father's slumming? To not even be worthy of acknowledgment? It festered in him like a slow-moving disease.

When Alex had sought him out weeks later, he had been teetering on the edge of darkness and light, his old life a seductive siren's call. Giovanni had made him choose. Embrace the chance you've been offered, he'd said, or forever cling to your anger. There is no in between.

The darkness he'd sensed in his grandfather, the raw acknowledgment he *knew* the dark side because he hadn't been able to pull his own son from it, had touched something inside Nate, perhaps the tiny sliver of hope he had left in him. He had chosen the light.

Blinking, he pulled himself out of the memory to focus on Mina's big dark eyes, the expression in them as adrift, as fear-driven, as his had been. She had no money, nowhere to go. She was as lost a soul as he had been. He couldn't let her fall through the cracks.

By the time they had landed in Capri a short while later, a plan had formed in his head. It would solve all his issues, except, of course, the ring on his finger. That, unfortunately, wasn't going anywhere.

Mina stood on the terrace of the penthouse suite of the Grand Hotel Emelia, the Bay of Marina Piccola sparkling in the distance. She had been to the glamorous island of Capri once with her family when she had been very young, six or seven. She only remembered bits and pieces of the holiday, but it was one of her best memories.

The beautiful beaches and the lovely walks along the coast had been her favorite activities, made extra special by the time she'd gotten to spend with her busy father, who'd taken a real holiday for once. They'd spent hours playing in the sand, digging sand castles and moats while her mother shopped and lunched with the jet-set crowd.

Her father had indulged her mother's every whim on the trip, including generous amounts of both his time and money. Her mother had, in turn, sparkled, and everything had been perfect for once. No arguments between her fiery parents that seemed to come all too frequently at home. Just sunshine and laughter.

She remembered playing with her favorite doll, Eva, on the beach with her father. Ankle-deep in the surf, she'd turned her back on the doll, only to find Eva gone when she turned around seconds later. Her father had spent the better part of an hour trying to retrieve the doll, understanding this was life or death for Mina. When he'd finally found her, laying a soaked, bedraggled Eva in her eager hands, he'd given her one of his stern lectures. "Take care of precious things, Mina. When they're gone, they're gone. I won't always be able to bring them back for you."

Her eyes burned as the glittering water of the bay she'd misplaced Eva in sparkled in the early-evening sun. How apropos her father's words had been. She'd lost him soon after that—her one grounding force.

Her lashes came down to shield her eyes from the

hot glow of the sun, a pang of longing rippling through her. How she wished he was here right now to make sense of everything. If he was, she would never have left her life to venture into the complete unknown. She wouldn't be married to a stranger, *"Bastien Nathaniel Brunswick,"* her marriage certificate had elaborated, who was apparently so wealthy he owned this five-star hotel the glitterati called home. She wouldn't be feeling so wholly, all-encompassingly *lost*.

She wrapped her arms around herself as a chill nipped at her skin, the heavenly scent of bougainvillea and campanula floating on the breeze. She didn't even own the clothes on her back. The expensive dress she was wearing was one Nate had sent down to the boutique for so she could get out of her wedding dress, a good thing because every time she looked at it she thought about Silvio and how furious he must be. How furious her mother must be.

Something Nate was apparently ascertaining as he made a litany of phone calls to *Dio* knew who to find out. Her pulse picked up, her blood thrumming through her veins. What could he possibly say to smooth things over? To fix the mess she'd created? To warn Silvio off?

Was he finishing off his role as hero by ensuring Silvio left her alone before he threw her out and said thank you, but no thank you? *I had only intended a twenty-four-hour marriage and a ring as compensation and this is way, way beyond that…*

A whiff of citrus filled her head just before a delicate silk wrap landed around her shoulders. She jumped as Nate reached around her to tie the silk into a loose knot.

"You're still jumpy." He leaned against the railing beside her, his gaze on her face.

"You caught me off guard." She looked down at the expensive-looking wrap he'd secured around her rather than stare at his smoldering good looks in a white T-shirt and a pair of dark jeans that molded themselves to his muscular thighs and long legs. "Another thing I can't pay you for."

A wry smile crossed his face. "I'm good for it, Mina. That much I know."

What didn't he know? What he was going to do with her? She pressed her lips together as her severely stressed imagination ran away with her. *Get a hold of yourself, Mina.*

"This is a magnificent property." She looked out at the yachts bobbing on the cerulean blue sea as the sun made its descent into the horizon. "You said you named it for your mother?"

He nodded.

"She is special, then?"

His lips curved, a genuine warmth filling his eyes. "Extraordinary."

She tilted her head to one side. "What makes her so extraordinary?"

"She was a single mother. She put me first every day of her life and kept me on the right path."

The bittersweet ache inside of her swelled larger. "You are very lucky to have a mother who cares so much for you."

"Yes."

"And your father?"

"He was never a part of our lives."

She studied the hard set of his jaw. The cold cast that had replaced the warmth in his eyes. Perhaps that was where some of the toughness surrounding this man came from.

She forced herself to ask the question she couldn't avoid. "Was it Silvio who came after us?"

"Yes. But you don't need to worry about him. I've taken care of it."

"How?" She turned to face him, panic clawing at her throat. "He must be beyond furious. To be humiliated like that in front of half the city… He will *want* to punish me."

"He *is* furious."

Her heart leaped into her mouth. "You *talked* to him?"

"Pasquale gave him my name. I stole his bride." He lifted a shoulder. "It was a necessary conversation."

"What did he *say*?"

"Nothing you need to know. Suffice it to say, he won't be bothering you again."

"Nate—"

"Stop." His gaze hardened. "He isn't a nice man, Mina, you knew that. He didn't have nice things to say. All you need to know is that I communicated the point that you are mine. You are safe from him. End of story."

She took a deep breath. Absorbed the deadly glimmer in his eyes. *Who was he* that he could so cavalierly tell Silvio Marchetti to call off the dogs and expect that he would? *Had* she jumped from the frying pan into the fire with him? Or did she trust Nate like she instinctively felt she could?

"What about my mother?" She'd been avoiding her calls to her mobile all day, with no idea what she'd even say if she did pick it up.

"She called me after I spoke with Silvio. Was *worried* about you, wanted to reassure herself you were okay." His smile was grim. "I told her you'd like a few days of privacy to enjoy our honeymoon and then you would call her."

Her mouth dropped open. "What else did you say?"

"That we are in love. That today was a mad, passionate impulse on our part." He lifted a broad shoulder. "It seemed as good a story as any to get Silvio off your back. I mentioned your cold feet were a product of our short but *intense* courtship."

Oh, mio Dio. She pressed her hands to her face. "You did not."

"I needed to give him a good reason to leave you alone, Mina. Now he has one. A man like Silvio would consider you used goods."

Used goods? She shook her head at the insanity of it all and paced to the end of the terrace. Now Silvio and her mother thought she had been intimate with Nate while she'd been engaged to Silvio. *Maledizione.* She didn't even want to think of how her mother had reacted. Or the harsh words that were undoubtedly on her voice mail.

"What did Silvio say to all this?"

"He said he was done with you. I said, *Good*. Because I'd take him apart if he came anywhere near you. So put your mind at ease, Mina. It's going to be fine."

Easier said than done. Her head spun as he disappeared inside and returned with a bottle of champagne and two glasses. She watched him warily as he uncorked the bottle. "I think the brandy was quite enough."

"You're wound tight as a bow." He worked the cork out of the bottle, a loud pop cutting through the air. "A glass of wine will help. And," he added, flicking her a glance from beneath dark lashes, "I have a proposition for you."

His request to deliver the Marc de Grazia Guardiola personally to his hotel room filled her head. He didn't mean—

"No, I don't mean that." His mouth twisted as he read her thoughts. "As much as I think *that* would loosen you up, what I have in mind involves another business proposition for you and I. Because like it or not, Mina, we are stuck together."

They were? Hope flared inside of her. "You're proposing we stay married?"

"I see no other option." He poured the champagne in the glasses. "As certain as I am that I got the message across to Silvio today that you are untouchable, I'm not about to set you loose on the streets of Capri like…an orphan searching for a home."

She frowned.

He waved a hand at her. "The point is I need that ring to show my grandfather. You need to be protected.

So we stay together for the year and, like our original plan, we both get what we need."

Relief flooded through her. "I don't want to be a burden. I could work for one of your hotels. Pay my way. I'm a very good chambermaid."

"You're smarter than that." He handed her a glass of champagne. "You proved to me what an innovative thinker you are that day at the Giarruso. You have great ideas, Mina. I'm offering to take you on as my protégée for the year."

"Protégée?" Her fingers tightened around the stem of the glass.

He nodded. "I own a chain of luxury hotels from one side of the globe to the other. The best of the best. If you want to learn about business I can teach you everything you need to know."

She frowned. "Why would you do that? I mean, I know you said I had good ideas, but surely you must be too busy for something like that?"

He leaned back against the railing, champagne glass in hand. "I got my start in business from someone who took a chance on me. I believe in paying it forward."

She thought about what few options she had—as in none without a cent to her name, without a home to go back to. She'd made a decision when she'd left with Nate: to stand on her own two feet; to not allow herself to be controlled by anyone anymore; to make her own way in the world. The only path left was forward.

Nate was offering her a chance to fulfill her dream—to follow in her father's footsteps. A once-in-a-lifetime opportunity to work with the best because he thought she was smart and had potential. Because he thought she was more than the pretty face her mother had always pegged her as.

A warm feeling spread through her, heat infusing her cheeks at the validation she had craved. To say the thought of becoming Nate's protégée was intimidating vastly understated the apprehension snaking through her insides. The combined terror and exhilaration the thought inspired. And yet she trusted him. Had instinctively trusted him this entire, crazy day. He hadn't blinked once at coming to her aid despite what she'd thrown at him. Yes, he wanted the ring, but there was more to it than that. He *cared* despite his tough exterior.

"I don't know what to say," she said finally. "You're an honorable man, Nate Brunswick. *Grazie.*"

"Not so honorable, Mina." A dark glitter entered his eyes. "You called me improper not so long ago. I can be that and more. I am a hard, ruthless businessman who does what it takes to make money. I will turn a hotel over in the flash of an eye if I don't see the flesh on the bones I envisioned when I bought it. I will enjoy a woman one night and send her packing the next when I get bored of her company. Know what you're getting into with me if you accept this. You will learn the dog-eat-dog approach to life, *not* the civilized one."

Why did something that was intended to be a warning send a curious shudder through her? Mina drew the wrap closer around her shoulders, her gaze tangling with Nate's. The glitter in his eyes stoked to a hot, velvet shimmer as he took a step forward and ran a finger along the line of her jaw. "Rule number one of this new arrangement, should you so choose to accept it, is to not look at me like that, *wife*. If we do this, we keep things strictly business so both of us walk away after the year with exactly what we want."

Her gaze fell away from his, her blood hot and thick in her veins. "You're misinterpreting me."

"No, I'm not." He brought his mouth to her ear, his warm breath caressing her cheek. "I have a hell of a lot more experience than you do, Mina. I can recognize the signs. They were loud and clear in my hotel room that day and they're loud and clear now."

She took a deep, shuddering breath. To protest further would be futile when her skin felt like it was on fire, her knees like jelly. He watched her like a cat played with a mouse, all powerful and utterly sure of himself. "The only thing that would be more of a disaster than this day's already been," he drawled finally, apparently ready to have mercy on her, "would be for us to end up in bed together. So a partnership it is, Mina." He lifted his glass. "What do you say?"

She seized hold of her senses. "So we have a marriage in name only and a business partnership. How are we positioning the marriage to others?"

"As if it's a real marriage." He shrugged. "I see no harm in that and there is the Silvio factor."

"And what about—" A wave of heat sped to her cheeks. "I mean, if we're not sleeping together, how will you—you know…?"

A wicked smile curved his mouth. "*Relieve myself?* There are ways. And if I choose to indulge, I'll do it discreetly."

Right. She dug her teeth into her bottom lip. Seized the moment. "Yes," she said, lifting her glass. "*Grazie*, Nate. I accept."

Her dark and apparently not so honorable husband pointed his glass at her. "Then tomorrow we begin. Get some good sleep tonight, Mina. You're going to need it for the ride I'm going to take you on."

CHAPTER FIVE

MINA DIDN'T SLEEP WELL. For hours she'd lain awake, terrified that despite Nate's assurances she was safe, Silvio would come after her. That perhaps his declaration it was over between them had just been to lull Nate into a false sense of complacency before he came after her to seek revenge.

"Refuse me again and you'll discover the depths to which my anger can sink. I will not tolerate you repeating any of your silly jitters to anyone, Mina."

She had trumped that. She had married another man!

She had little time to nurse her coffee over breakfast with Nate, however, her brain barely awake when he hit her with his Business Rule Number One. "You only get one chance to make a first impression. *Looking* the part is the first step to realizing the role."

She couldn't disagree with that, because clad in a silver-gray suit with an ice-blue tie, handmade Italian shoes gleaming on his feet, Nate looked every bit the power broker that he was. So off she went with Susana, the manager of the hotel's boutique, to outfit herself with a casual and business wardrobe.

Susana had opened the boutique early just for them. She installed Mina in a chair in the fitting area with a tablet and coffee while she and an assistant gathered clothes. Mina used the time to research her enigmatic husband, hoping for some clues as to what made him tick.

It turned out to be a rather useless activity, because none of the business profiles she pulled up on Nate delved into anything more personal than she already knew. The grandson of legendary shipping tycoon Giovanni Di Sione, he had worked his way up the ranks of Di Sione Shipping, eventually running various overseas branches of the company before leaving to start Brunswick Developments, his multibillion-dollar real-estate development firm.

A self-made man who has used his uncanny business acumen, aggressive street smarts and brutal negotiating tactics to land marquee deals that put him on the Forbes *billionaires list at age thirty-four.*

Giving in to an urge she couldn't suppress, she typed in her husband's name plus the word *woman*. A slew of photos came up. True to his word, the majority of his dates at the high-society events he frequented were brunettes, with a few blondes of late. All stunning. All vastly more sophisticated than her.

"Ready?" Susana bustled into the changing area

with another armful of clothes. Mina put the tablet down and got to her feet to take half the pile.

"Can I give you some advice?" the other woman said, glancing down at the tablet. "Don't do that. A man like Nate is going to have a past. You'll only torture yourself."

Heat scored her cheeks. "I will say congratulations on doing the impossible," continued Susana as she hung up the suits. "Mingmei will undoubtedly be wondering how you did it."

"Mingmei?"

"The manager of our Hong Kong hotel. Better you know about *that* one before you come face-to-face with her. Mingmei and Nate had an affair before she came to work for him."

"How long ago was that?"

"Three years ago. Clearly it ended well because he hired her, but Mingmei—"

"—still desires Nate."

"Perhaps." Susana handed her a cream-colored suit. "How did you and Nate meet?"

Mina's brain worked furiously. "We met at the hotel in Sicily where I worked. In the bar. It was…love at first sight."

Susana smiled. "*That* I would have liked to have seen. It would have been entertaining to watch the Ice Man fall."

Mina diverted the conversation to clothes after that before she stumbled over another answer. Three hours of endless fittings later, she walked out of the boutique the owner of a stylish, power-based wardrobe with some pretty things for the evening. "You'll need it," Susana had advised. "Nate's social calendar is daunting."

Her phone rang as she walked back across the courtyard. She glanced at the screen, her stomach doing a slow churn. *Her mother.* Maybe it was better to get it out of the way.

She sat on a bench and took the call. "*Ciao*, Mamma."

There was silence on the other end of the line. Then, *"Che pensi che stai facendo,* Mina*?"* What do you think you're doing?

Her cheeks fired, her fingers trembling around the phone. "I couldn't marry Silvio, Mamma. I told you that but you wouldn't listen."

"So you disgraced your fiancé, this *family*, in front of the entire city?"

She bit her lip. "He hit me. I can't live with a man like that."

"And you expect your American tycoon to be any different? Men are all the same. They want a beautiful wife on their arm who obeys them, Mina. Who *uncomplicates* their life. Start disagreeing with your American after the rosy glow is over and see how he acts."

"Nate would never hit me."

A pause. "Where are you now?"

She chewed hard on her lip.

Her mother made a strangled sound. "What will you do? Go live with him in America? You will surely have to now, because your reputation is in tatters. This *family's* reputation is in tatters."

A lump formed in her throat. She didn't even know where Nate lived. Only that it was in New York.

"Mi dispiace," she murmured huskily. "You left me no choice, Mamma."

"You disappoint me, Mina."

What was new about that? She had always disappointed her mother. Had never understood why when she'd done everything asked of her. Had attained top grades at school, had dated her endless contingent of bachelors, and still been found lacking.

"What about our plan? To sell the ring?"

Her heart sank. There it was. What her mother truly cared about. "It hasn't changed. I will sell the ring and pay off our debts. But as I'm sure Pasquale told you, I can't do that for a year."

"Perhaps," her mother said deliberately, "your husband could help."

She closed her eyes. "I won't ask that of him, Mamma."

There was silence on the other end of the line. There would be no inquiry as to how she was. Whether she was happy. None of that mattered to her mother. Had never. "I have to go," she said thickly.

"Mina—"

She ended the call. A deep, all-encompassing throb moved through her. Made it hard to breathe. She'd gotten past her naïveté about her mother a long time ago. It was the depth to which she didn't care that shocked her now.

She was alone in this world. Utterly alone. Her life would have to be shaped by her and her alone.

* * *

Nate had just finished reviewing the financials for the Emelia when Mina walked through the door in a charcoal-gray suit, her traffic-stopping legs clad in a pair of finely made Italian heels.

If he'd thought a suit would help dull his attraction to her he had been entirely wrong. The suit was conservative, covered all the requisite parts adequately; it was what was under it that was unavoidable. The fitted jacket highlighted her tiny waist and taut high breasts, the knee-length pencil skirt skimmed generous hips.

A power suit to be sure, but on his wife it swayed all the power in favor of her innate sensuality.

He brought his gaze back up to her face. Studied the pallor that blanched her honey-colored skin. "What's wrong? Did Silvio contact you?"

She set down the bag she was holding and slid off her shoes. "No—it's—I'm fine."

"You were having nightmares about it last night. You're not fine."

A flush filled her cheeks. "I woke you?"

"I was still working. Mina, I promised to protect you and I will. You don't need to worry about him."

"I know. I do. It's just—sometimes my imagination gets the better of me." She raked her hair out of her face. "That's not why I'm upset. My mother called. She was furious. Not that I hadn't expected that. My reputation is in tatters. Also not surprising."

"Then why the lost look? What did she say to you?"

She shook her head. "You are my boss now. I should keep this professional."

He gave her a wry look. "We are also married. I think we have a rather unique relationship. What did she say?"

She exhaled. "She wasn't worried about me. She didn't ask if I was okay. She didn't care if I was happy with you. She said I'd disappointed her."

He lifted a brow. "For running away from a monster to marry a man who professes to love you and will keep you safe? For delivering the exact same result in the sale of the ring? What kind of a mother is she?"

She shook her head. "She never wanted children. My father did. I was always with my nanny, Camilla. As soon as my father died, she sent me off to boarding school in France, as if she couldn't wait to get rid of me. I always came home with good grades, top of my class, but it seemed inconsequential to her. She just didn't care."

"How old were you when your father died?"

"Eight."

The image of a tiny Mina being sent off to school at such a young age pulled at his heartstrings. "You've never talked to her about it? Asked her why?"

She lifted a shoulder. "My *mamma*—she is cold. It's her way. I told myself to let it go. To not wish for the impossible. But sometimes I do. I wish I knew what she finds so…*lacking* in me so I can fix it."

He knew how that felt. To always wonder what it was about you that was so defective your own father wanted nothing to do with you. That he could turn his back on his own flesh and blood and slam a door in your face when you had come to beg for assistance. To deny you even existed. But he knew it was a fruitless pursuit. A soul-destroying pursuit.

"It's better not to wonder," he told Mina roughly, "to look for that flaw in yourself you think they see in you. Because it's not you, it's her. She should have been a proper mother to you and she wasn't. That's her cross to bear, not yours. Don't waste your life trying to figure out something you'll likely never get an answer to."

She blinked. "Are you talking about your father?"

He ignored that. "Learn how to stand on your own two feet. How to exist without her approval. It will be the most empowering thing you can ever do."

She nodded, but hurt still throbbed in her eyes.

He sighed. "What?"

"She's all I have."

His heart squeezed. "You're better off without her. That's not how a true parent acts."

Her mouth compressed. Turning on her heel, she walked into her bedroom, came back and handed him the massive diamond solitaire Silvio had given her. "I need to give this back."

He took the small fortune out of her hands. "I'll have it sent to him. Speaking of which, we'll need to get you a rock for show."

"It's not necessary."

"You're my wife, Mina, it is. People will be looking."

She sat down on the sofa and poured herself a cup of coffee. "Susana asked me how we met. I was unprepared for the question. I told her we met in the bar at the Giarruso. It was the first response that came to me."

His mouth curved. "That I picked you, extraordinarily innocent Mina, up in a hotel bar after work?" He sat down on the sofa opposite her. "Seems a stretch but we'll go with it."

"I should know a few pertinent details about you if we're to carry this off. It was awkward with Susana."

He lifted a brow. "Such as?"

"Where do you live in New York?"

"I have a penthouse off Central Park in the heart of Manhattan. It's not as beautiful as Sicily, but I think you'll enjoy the energy of the city."

"You said we're not going back to New York right away?"

"We have week-long stops in Hong Kong and the Maldives after Capri, then we head home."

She blinked at the blindingly fast pace of her new life. "Brothers or sisters?"

"I have seven half siblings from my father's marriage."

"Are you close to them?"

What to say? That he and his brothers and sisters were perhaps the most dysfunctional clan on the planet? That there was not only a deep wedge between himself and Alex, but a distance he kept with all of them because every single one of them was a bit broken from their past and it was easier not to open up old wounds?

"I'm not sure I'd characterize it as close," he said finally, "but we do interact from time to time."

"I know you run and like the opera, but do you have any other hobbies? Other leisure activities I should know of that are a passion?"

His mouth twisted. "Work is my passion. I work fourteen-…fifteen-hour days, Mina. Not much time for anything else. Which," he suggested, "is what we should focus on now. Unless you have more questions?"

She shook her head. "That will do for now."

He picked up the report on the Emelia's financials and handed it to her. "Review this. We'll talk it over after you've had a chance to read it, but first I want to go over the ground rules of how we'll work together."

She crossed her legs primly and sat back to listen.

"First of all," he said, "you are here to learn. So learn. The most valuable thing you can do over the next year is to sit back and listen, soak up everything that's being said, conduct your own analysis, and afterward, when it's just the two of us, you can ask any questions you may have.

"Secondly, I want you to watch the people in this meeting or any meeting we're in. Watch their body language, look for their nonverbal cues, because they are often more telling than what is coming out of their mouth. Always look for an angle, because *everyone* has an angle in business, an agenda they're walking into the room with. Understanding these goals and different agendas is a crucial skill in any negotiation—antagonistic or friendly."

"I've been told my father was brilliant with people." A proud light entered Mina's eyes. "He once solved a strike that had been going on for weeks at one of our plants by walking into the picket lines and hashing out a deal with the workers."

"Which translates into my third rule," said Nate. "I

JENNIFER HAYWARD   85

want you to be a problem solver. Come to me with a solution, not an issue."

She nodded. *"Bene."*

"That's it for now." He nodded toward the report. "Profits have been sagging over the past year at the Emelia. We need to light a fire under things. See what you think."

The meeting with Giorgio and the Emelia management team went worse than Nate had expected. Complacency had set in at the hotel and it seemed his general manager had no plan how to lift sagging profits because he didn't think he *had* a problem.

"The market is down, Nate," Giorgio soothed in that smooth-as-silk voice of his. "We're doing everything we can to entice new customers to the hotel, but we can't *manufacture* them."

Nate directed a look at Mina. "Was the Giarruso's occupancy rate down this year?"

She frowned. "Not much. I think the manager said five percent."

"And you are down fifteen percent," Nate said to Giorgio.

Giorgio put his hand on Mina's arm as if she were a child in need of correction. "It must have been more than five percent. Perhaps you have the numbers wrong."

"No," said Mina. "It was nowhere near fifteen percent."

Giorgio sat back and crossed his arms over his chest. "What do you propose I do? Alter the economies of the western world? Manipulate the markets? We've upped the sales and marketing budgets. The effort is there, Nate."

"The effort is *ineffective*."

Giorgio's face reddened. Silence fell at the table.

"What about repeat guests?" Mina interjected. "Your number is way down. What if you—"

Nate shot her a withering look. She sat back in her chair and closed her mouth.

"What is your plan of attack for them?" Nate asked Giorgio.

"We've done a whole discounted rate campaign. It isn't moving rooms."

"Then it isn't compelling enough."

Giorgio looked at Mina. "What were you going to suggest?"

Nate nodded tightly at her to go ahead.

"I was thinking of a 'remember the memories' type campaign," Mina said. "I was here in Capri on holidays with my family years ago. When we arrived it brought back such great memories. So perhaps something more emotion based than financial."

Giorgio steepled his hands together. "I like it."

Nate liked it, too, but wished the idea had come from his manager and not his protégée. He continued to grill his top man until the end of the three-hour meeting, then mercifully ended it, ushering Mina up to their suite in tight-lipped silence.

"I know," Mina said in a preemptive strike, the minute the door closed behind them, "I wasn't supposed to talk. It's just it was getting *painful* and I had an idea."

"Painful is *good*. Discomfort shakes people up and pushes them outside of their comfort zone. Which, quite frankly, Giorgio needs desperately right now or he will be out of a job."

Her eyes widened, color washing her cheeks. "I thought by offering up an idea, Giorgio might build on it."

"And by doing so you *undermined* my attempt to teach him a lesson. After I told you not to talk." Nate pinned his gaze on her. "When I put someone in the hot seat I'm doing it for a reason, Mina. So keep your mouth *shut*."

She took a step back. "*Mi dispiace.* I—I didn't realize that's what you were doing. It won't happen again."

"No, it won't," he agreed, his voice sharp as a knife. "Because you will stick to my rules or you won't play at all."

She nodded rapidly, pupils as big as saucers, hands clenched by her sides. He did a double take. *She was afraid of him?*

Then he remembered what she'd just gone through... How intimidating he must look to her at twice her size towering over her. Furious. Mina wasn't one of his toughened, worldly employees used to his rants. She was a baby chick who'd just taken fledgling steps out of the nest.

He shoved his hands in his pockets and blew out a breath. "Business isn't the glorified interaction of a tea party, where everyone plays nice and leaves with a smile on their face. It's a ferociously competitive playground where only the strongest survive. I could leave you in a back office, give you research work and not let you experience what it's really like, but that's no way to learn. So find yourself a thick skin, Mina. Learn to be a gladiator, because people's feelings don't matter in this game."

A determined glint entered her eyes as the fear faded from her face. "I can and I will, Nate. I apologize again. I did not mean to undermine your authority."

"Fine." He nodded. "Go get changed for the party."

She started toward her room.

"Mina?"

She turned around. "I thought your idea about the repeat guests was right on the money. Emotional affinity is the reason people will spend money in a downturn. I'm going to direct Giorgio to investigate with his marketing team."

Her face brightened. It was like the sun had come out. "*Grazie*, Nate."

His lips curved. "We'll see if you're still saying that after a month with me."

CHAPTER SIX

"WILL THIS DO?"

Nate shifted his gaze from the smartphone he'd been perusing to the spectacular set of legs in front of him. Moved up past rounded hips outlined in a shimmering midnight blue fabric to a modestly covered but spectacularly presented cleavage. The term *less is more* came to mind. With Mina less was always more. A man could be forgiven for concluding she was best left entirely unclothed for his undeniable pleasure.

And yet Mina, it seemed, had no idea of just how stunning she was, a fact that only increased her appeal. Lip caught between her teeth, a finger twirling a curl around it, her gaze on his for approval, it amused him to think of what her response would have been had he suggested what would have been on his mind had she been his wife in more than name.

Her eyes on his in the ornate mirror on the wall, her palms flat on the antique table in front of it, her dress around her waist as he put that *just taken* glow in her cheeks that marked her his.

Mina's eyes widened. Her lashes came down to fan her cheeks.

"You look stunning," he said, before he shocked her from here to New York. "The color suits you."

"Grazie." She smoothed the dress over her hips. "So tell me the goal for the evening."

She was learning. "The Grand Hotel chain," he said, tucking his smartphone into the pocket of his jacket, "has partnered with Hollywood legends Antonio Davis and Franco Messini on a series of nightclubs located in select properties around the world—London, LA, Capri and New York. Curious—the nightclub brand—reflects the exclusive, adventurous cross section of clientele who frequent it and the unique experiences the nightclub offers."

"I know Antonio Davis," Mina said, her eyes shining. "He's a legend. I love his movies."

"He's also a shrewd businessman. Brilliant at extending his brand to other realms. Tonight," he said, buttoning his jacket, "is the opening night for Curious in Capri. Antonio and Franco have flown their entourages in for the event, the goal to stir up excitement for the launch."

"And what will be the unique experience tonight, then?"

"It's an Arabian Nights theme. Exotic, sensual. All the usual decor. But there will also be a tattoo artist who is doing henna tattoos. It's a unique branding opportunity guests will show off after the event, keeping the buzz going."

"Henna tattoos are all the rage in the magazines."

"I think they look very sexy on a woman." He arched a brow at her. "Have you tried?"

"I don't think it's really me."

"You never know until you try." The wicked note to his voice brought a pretty pink flush to her cheeks. "Antonio's entourage is fine to mingle with, by the way. Franco's can be questionable. Steer clear of them."

She nodded, a flicker of something he couldn't read in her eyes.

"What?"

"You think I'm hopelessly naive."

His mouth tipped up at one corner. "Aren't you?"

She stared at him for a long moment, the flush in her cheeks increasing, then bent to retrieve her wrap from a chair. "Who am I supposed to be this evening? Your protégée or your pretend wife?"

"My jaw-droppingly beautiful wife." He swiped the wrap from her and draped it around her shoulders, his fingertips brushing against her enticing golden skin. "The big bad wolves are coming out to play tonight, Mina. Thus the warning."

She lifted her chin. "I've attended more society parties than I'd care to count. I'll be fine."

"Not like this one."

Her gaze lowered to his hands, still resting on her bare shoulders, as if she wondered why they were still there. He wondered, too. Wondered why every excuse to touch her was irresistible.

Perhaps the wolves were inside, too…

His hands slid from her shoulders. "Tonight will be a good dry run for you for New York. The news that we're married will filter back to the press. They'll be all over us for a bit, I expect."

An apprehensive look entered her beautiful brown eyes. He pressed his palm to her back and propelled her to the door. "You're a gladiator, remember? This is a piece of cake."

The Curious party, held in the Emelia's sleek outdoor lounge that overlooked the bay, was in full swing when they arrived. To the outward eye it looked as if it had been flawlessly executed by Giorgio's staff. Arabian Nights–style tents in vibrant jeweled colors blanketed the furniture-strewn space, varying in size and complexity. Gauzy green and purple curtains, both drawn and open, hinted at two degrees of interaction, both social and seductively intimate.

The interior of the tents was over-the-top fantasy, those same jeweled tones reflected in the pillows and throws that covered the low-slung divans and rich tapestries. Copious amounts of candles, ornate lamps, bejeweled belly dancers giving partygoers seductive performances and the tattoo artists completed the ambience. It was as if you'd just made your way through the desert and stumbled upon an oasis filled with the most beautiful people on earth.

Jewels were abundant, paid escorts, too, accompanying the rich men who required a beautiful woman by their side.

"Paid escorts?" Mina didn't seem to get the concept. "You mean *prostitutes*?"

"I doubt they would appreciate that terminology,"

he drawled. "I expect some will provide recreational activity and some are here for appearances only."

"Oh." She shut up after that as he networked his way through the space with ruthless efficiency. He wasn't a natural-born socializer. It was a means to an end, a necessary requirement of the job. His wife, on the other hand, was in her element, circulating with an effortless poise, murmuring polite phrases in that sexy Italian lilt of hers, adjusting to the interests and personality of everyone that she met on the fly to put them perfectly at ease. He found himself captivated by her charm, by the chameleon that she was, his attention focused on her with an unwavering fascination that was a new experience for him.

Antonio Davis separated himself from the crowd when he saw them, drawing his longtime Hollywood starlet of a girlfriend, Evangelina, toward them. Antonio wrapped an arm around Nate and gave him a slap on the back. "Heard you were here. Also heard you were *married* to this stunning creature. What gives? No invitation?"

"We married rather…impulsively yesterday or you most certainly would have been invited." Nate nodded at Mina. "Mina meet Antonio Davis and his other half, Evangelina Cabriera."

Antonio gave Mina a kiss on both cheeks as did Evangelina. Mina gave the actor a shy look. "I love your films. I learned to speak English with your movies."

The aging Hollywood heartthrob, whose outward cool masked the intensely ambitious, genuinely likeable guy he was inside, smiled. "So one of your first phrases was, 'Shoot 'em up, Charlie'?"

"I think it was actually, 'I'm no hero, kid. I'm just a man with a good horse and impeccable timing.'"

Antonio threw back his head, a deep booming laugh escaping him. The cowboy lingo delivered in Mina's sexy Italian accent didn't quite have the same ring to it. "Liked Carson, did you?"

"Loved him. It was so fun watching him discover Charlie was a girl."

"Fun role to play." Antonio lifted a brow at Nate. "Seen Franco?"

"Not yet."

Antonio grimaced. "He's been *otherwise occupied.*"

Nate didn't want to know what that might be. Hollywood's resident bad boy didn't seem to recognize he was far past the age where he should be doing all-nighters with copious amounts of illegal drugs. He dealt with Antonio and left Franco out of it and they ran a squeaky clean business together.

"Any interest in joining Evangelina for a tattoo?" Antonio asked Mina. "She's dying to have one and I have a bit of business I wanted to discuss with Nate."

Mina looked to Nate for confirmation. He gave her a challenging glance that said, *Expand your horizons.* Mina's chin lifted. "I'd love to."

Antonio filled him in on the new business idea he had for a stand-alone series of nightclubs. Nate liked it immediately. Liked even more that Franco was not involved. "Send the proposal over."

"You got it." The actor smiled and waved at someone. "Hey, there's a financier here you should meet."

He scanned the crowd for Mina. She and Evangelina were in the middle of Franco's crowd. His gaze narrowed on Franco in a flashy white suit, his megawatt predatory smile fixed firmly on Mina.

"She's a big girl," Antonio said, sliding an arm around his shoulders. "She'll be fine."

Mina was trying to relax and enjoy herself, she really was. But this party was like nothing she'd ever experienced before. Evangelina was throwing back drinks twice as fast as she was and introducing her around to famous actors, actresses and producers at such a pace her head spun. She was afraid she was going to insult somebody by not remembering them and the men seemed inordinately *friendly*, their admiring eyes seeming to linger just a bit too long.

The buzzing atmosphere only heightened the chaotic feeling inside of her the last twenty-four hours had induced. Walking away from her home, that awful phone call with her mother this afternoon, Nate's anger at her for overstepping her bounds in that meeting. She would have preferred to be curled up in their suite watching one of Antonio's Westerns.

"Hey, beautiful." Franco Messini took advantage of a break in Evangelina's watch over her to grab her hand and lead her to the bar.

"I don't really need another glass of wine."

"Can't leave my lovely guest empty-handed," Franco purred, raising his hand to signal the bartender. Securing them two glasses of champagne, he directed her away from the crowd at the bar. "I heard you say you were a fan of Sybil Atkinson. I just saw her. Let me introduce you to her."

Mina thought that was a fine idea. The less interaction she had with Franco alone, the better.

He led her through the crowd toward one of the tents. She followed him inside the small, intimate space with its seductive dim lighting. It was empty.

"I guess she moved on," she said lightly. "I really should get back to my husband. He's likely looking for me."

"He should be keeping closer tabs on you." Franco moved closer, his bulky body blocking out the light. The suspicious shimmer in his blue eyes sent a frisson of unease through her. She wondered if he'd been indulging in more than just alcohol. "You're the most beautiful woman at this party, Mina."

She licked dry lips as he continued to move closer. "That's very nice of you to say. But I really think I should get back to Nate."

"In a minute." Franco ran a finger down the bare skin of her upper arm. "It isn't a crime to look at another man's wife, is it?"

But he was *touching* her. She took a step backward, the unsettled feeling inside of her unraveling into alarm. Her palms sweaty, pulse racing in her throat, she swallowed hard. "I'd like to get back to the others."

"Don't look so threatened." Franco's confident, aggressive gaze mocked her as he closed the space between them again. "You haven't given me the time of day since we met. I just want to get to know you better. You are my business partner's wife, after all."

"I don't think that's a good idea. My husband—he—he's the jealous sort."

The actor lifted a hand and ran a finger down her cheek. "Maybe he should learn to share... Nate's always been a smug bastard. Too much so for my taste."

Her pulse pounded harder, her palms growing ice cold now. She darted a glance at the exit, blocked by Franco's big body. Told herself to stay calm. But an image of Silvio manacling her wrist, kissing her, the crack of his hand snapping her head sideways, sent her heart slamming against her chest.

Franco was so much bigger than her.

The air in the tent seemed to dissolve. Her breath came faster, tighter, intensifying the cloudy feeling in her head.

"Please—" she murmured in a broken tone.

Franco dragged his thumb across the edge of her jaw. "Please what?"

Please let me go.

"You'd best be taking your hands off my wife."

Nate's voice, low and tight, cut through the air. Franco turned, revealing her husband silhouetted in the light, standing just inside the entrance to the tent. His gaze was trained on the actor, a quiet, white-hot fury on his face.

Franco eyed Nate. He was equally as tall as the actor, but less bulky, with more lean-packed muscle. Ferociously intimidating in the way he carried it. Franco registered it, too, apparently, for he stepped back, hands raised. "Easy, Brunswick. We were just talking."

"Which explains why my wife looks petrified." Nate walked to Mina and slid an arm around her. She leaned into him, her knees going weak.

"You try my patience, Franco." Nate fixed his gaze on the actor. "Clean up your act or I will end this partnership, no matter how much I like Antonio."

Franco scowled. "You have far too much invested to do that."

"*Watch me.* Get lost, Messini. You ever come within ten feet of my wife again and I will take you apart."

Franco's belligerent gaze tangled with Nate's. For a heart-stopping minute she wasn't sure which way it was going to go. Then Franco turned on his heel and left.

Mina sagged with relief. Nate turned her around, keeping his arm banded around her waist. "What happened?"

She shook her head. "Nothing—he—I should never have allowed him to bring me here. He said he was going to introduce me to Sybil Atkinson, but when we arrived, there was no one here."

His mouth flattened. "I told you not to mess with Franco or his crowd."

"I wasn't. I was avoiding him. Then Evangelina went off to talk to someone and he just swooped in."

"What did he say to you?"

She frowned. "Something just seemed *off* in the way he was looking at me. I told him I wanted to go, but he wouldn't let me… He started touching me. He said it wasn't a crime to look at another man's wife.

That—" her chin dipped "—you were a smug bastard who should learn to share."

Black heat shimmered in his eyes. "He said *that*?"

"Sì." Her stomach clenched at the sudden stillness in his tall, lean body. "I'm sure it was all, what do you Americans call it? *Bravado?*" she said hurriedly. "That I was overreacting. I—I saw Silvio in my head. I went back to the night he hit me and I froze. I told myself to walk away, to come find you, but my legs wouldn't work."

The aggression in his gaze softened. "It's common for a person put into a threatening situation to freeze. To shut down." He shook his head. "It's my fault. I should never have left you alone with this crowd."

He wrapped his fingers around hers. "Let's go."

She followed him out of the tent. Balked when he headed toward the exit. "I don't want to ruin your evening. I've already caused enough problems between you and Franco."

"Franco and I already had issues. And *you* did not cause that scene. Franco did." He put a hand to her back and propelled her through the crowd. "I was coming to find you to leave."

The lights of Capri glimmered around them as they rode the glass elevator up to their penthouse suite. She started to feel silly as she studied Nate's grim face. She had totally overreacted. Franco hadn't really been a threat. He'd been trying to push Nate's buttons. *Hers.* And she had let him.

Nate was probably wondering what in *Dio*'s name he'd signed on for with her.

"You okay?"

She sighed. "I feel like you're always rescuing me. You must think I'm some kind of damsel in distress who can't take care of herself."

He shook his head. "This was my fault tonight, Mina."

"No. It's just—" She bit her lip. "I'm not normally like this."

"What are you normally like?"

She lifted a shoulder. "Self-sufficient. Strong. I was eight when I was sent to that boarding school in France. I didn't speak the language. I was brutally lonely. I learned to be a survivor."

"You are," he pointed out. "You could have allowed yourself to be a victim with Silvio. You could have married him and suffered a lifetime of abuse. But you didn't. That took guts."

She nodded. It's just that she hated that person she'd been tonight. Hated *everything* being so out of her control. That she couldn't seem to trust her instincts anymore.

"You've had your life turned upside down over the past forty-eight hours, Mina." Nate rested his gaze on her face. "Cut yourself some slack. You need to honor your fear as well as put it behind you when you're ready."

He was right. She knew that.

"Have you ever considered taking martial arts?"

She frowned. "I'm not sure it's my thing."

"You should consider it. It's very empowering for a woman to learn how to defend herself."

"Do you do it?"

He nodded. "Karate."

"How good are you?"

"A black belt. But you don't have to be skilled to defend yourself. You just need to know the basics."

"That's very impressive," she told him as he guided her off the elevator and into the penthouse. *Also sexy.*

He undid his jacket and shrugged it off. "I grew up in a rough neighborhood. I needed to protect myself. There were two ways to do that—with weapons or as your own personal weapon. I eventually chose karate."

"Eventually?"

His dark lashes fanned down over his cheeks. "I had a few iffy years before I made that choice."

She absorbed that piece of new information. She'd imagined being a Di Sione or half of one would have meant being brought up in luxury. The fact that he hadn't had an entitled upbringing seemed to better reflect the man. The uncivilized edge beneath the veneer Franco had taken one look at tonight and walked away from.

He threw her a glance as he loosened his tie and undid the top couple of buttons of his shirt. "So? I could sign you up for some classes at my gym in New York."

"I don't know," she said dubiously. "I'm not a very physical person."

"You're a gladiator, remember?"

Not much of one tonight.

"I can show you how you would have gotten out of that situation with Silvio if that would make you feel better."

Her brow creased. "How? He's far bigger than me."

"If you knew self-defense, you could have. Show me what happened that night. I'll teach you a couple of simple self-defense techniques."

"Now?"

He gave her an amused look. "Now."

She chewed on her lip. The desire to take back control, to wipe the fear from her head, was too strong to resist. "*Sì*. Please show me."

He nodded. "Tell me what happened that night."

"We were in my mother's salon. I had just poured Silvio a drink. He was angry with me for telling him I had cold feet about the marriage. He—he grabbed my wrist and pulled me toward him and started kissing me. I was…surprised. He hadn't been aggressive with me before. The kiss—it started to get…*intimo*." Her gaze dropped away from his. "I didn't like it so I tried to push him away, but he wouldn't let me go. Then he hit me across the face."

Nate stepped toward her. "Show me how close you were to him."

She stared at him. "What?"

"I need to know how far apart you were. How much room you had to maneuver. That determines what self-defense techniques you use."

"Oh." She thought back. "We were very close."

"Like this?" He took her wrist and pulled her to him. The brush of his tall strong body against hers sent heat rushing to her cheeks. Every nerve ending in her body flickered to life, making her so utterly aware of him she could hardly look at him.

"Maybe this isn't such a good idea," she murmured.

"*Show me*, Mina."

"We were closer than this."

"How close?"

She stepped into him until every centimeter of their bodies were touching from chest to knee. Her breasts brushed against his chest, her hips rested in the cradle of his, and *Dio mio*, this was not good. He was too overwhelmingly male. And she was having the opposite reaction to him than she'd had to Silvio.

"Where were his arms?"

"One was on my waist—well lower," she corrected hesitantly. "The other, I don't remember."

Nate slid his arm around her waist. "We'll go with this. This about right the way we're standing?"

"Sì."

He lowered his head and brought his mouth to within a centimeter of hers.

Her heart stuttered. "What are you doing?"

"Push me away."

Right. Dannazione, Mina—focus. She lifted her hand and pushed hard against his shoulder. It was like trying to move a brick wall.

"When you are this close," he told her, "you lose power. You have no room to maneuver. You either have to make space so you can attack him, which you aren't going to be able to do in this situation, or go for the vulnerable points."

"Vulnerable points?"

"My groin," he said pointedly. "Try bringing your knee up hard and fast."

"No."

"You're a gladiator."

She gritted her teeth and tried to lift her leg. She got exactly nowhere.

"Not enough room, right?"

She shook her head.

"What are my other vulnerable points?"

"Your face?"

"Be more specific."

"Your eyes?"

"And what else?"

"Your nose?"

"Yes, but the throat is better. A quick, hard strike against the throat—the Adam's apple of a man in particular—is perfect. It shocks me enough to let you go. Gouging at the eyes is also good. Your goal is to stun me long enough to get away."

She nodded.

"Let's try it from the beginning."

"The beginning?"

"You need to put yourself back in the scenario. Imagine it's happening, remember the sequence and go for one of my vulnerable points. I won't know which way you're going to go, which gives you the element of surprise that you would have in that situation."

She pressed her lips together. "Okay."

He slid an arm around her waist and tugged her close. "Ready?"

"Sì."

He brought his mouth down to hers, and this time he kissed her. Unlike the first kiss he'd given her in front of the registrar, this one was unavoidable, *dominant*, meant to simulate the one Silvio had given her. She trusted Nate. She did. Her heart pounded, anyway, at how helpless she felt. How much stronger he was. When he took the kiss deeper, made a claim on her she wasn't willing to submit to, she stiffened, gathered her strength and slammed her right hand hard in his throat.

Nate released her, his hands lifting to his throat. "Nice job," he rasped, half coughing, half speaking. "I expected you to go for the eyes."

Mina stared at him, hands clenched by her sides, adrenaline racing through her. "Are you okay?"

"Fine." His gaze narrowed. "The kiss was necessary, Mina. It had to be real. To evoke the violent reaction it did in you so you could use your power."

She nodded.

"And what did you do?"

"I got away."

"What would you have done next?"

"Run."

"Where?"

"Out the front door. The house was empty."

"Exactly," he said. "Move toward people. Help."

She unclenched her fists. Took a deep breath as she attempted to calm her body down.

"You've just taken back your power, Mina." Nate stepped toward her. "I *knew* the blow was coming and you still incapacitated me long enough for you to get away."

She nodded. Instructed her pounding heart to relax because this was Nate in front of her, not Silvio.

"If you have that power," he said, "you can choose who you trust. You can choose what situations you put yourself in. Not all men are violent. Some would only want to kiss you for pleasure—yours and their own."

She knew that. But the way she'd felt when Nate had just kissed her...

"What?"

She put a hand to her heart. "This *panic*. I know I can trust you and still I felt terrified."

"Like I said. Give yourself some time."

She forced a smile. "You're right. I just hate giving him that power over me."

He was silent for a long moment. "Then don't."

She blinked. *"Scusi?"*

"You trust me?"

She nodded.

"Then get back on the wagon." He took another step toward her, stopping just short of her personal space. "We're attracted to each other, Mina. Intensely attracted to each other. But I am not Silvio. I can kiss a woman and walk away, no matter how hot and bothered I am, regardless of where my emotions lie, because I am in control of them. I would never hurt a woman. So," he said deliberately, "kiss me right now. Replace that image of what happened with Silvio with a positive experience."

She gaped at him. "We can't do that. We made a rule."

"So we break it for one kiss. The longer you let this eat away at you, the harder it's going to be to leave behind."

She had a feeling that was true. She didn't want

to carry this victim mentality with her. Didn't want to give it a chance to take hold. Because this Mina Mastrantino she'd been tonight was not the real Mina. The Mina who had chased away her childish ghosts in boarding school because there'd been no one else to do it for her. The Mina who'd learned to survive without love when it seemed like everyone around her had it but her, by telling herself someday she would have it, too. The Mina who was stronger than this.

"Sì," she said. "Let's do it."

"Come here."

For a brief, heart-stopping moment, Mina thought she might actually be insane. Because this man was dangerous. Beautifully, undeniably, self-admittedly dangerous. Yet, she conceded, she trusted him implicitly.

He was letting her take control. He wouldn't make the first move.

She took a step forward, then another, until she was almost touching him. There she stopped, her innate shyness kicking in. Nate's gaze caught hers, pulled her in. She took the last step forward, sucking in a breath as he reached out, curved a hand around her waist and brought her to him in a loose hold that continued to give her every option.

She thought he would lean down and kiss her then. Instead, he focused on her lips, as if they were the most fascinating thing in the world. As if he had all the *time* in the world. Her breathing quickened, anticipation firing her blood. He brought his mouth down to hers without touching. Their breath mingled first, then the lush surfaces of their mouths. *Oh, mio Dio.* She was practically panting by the time he angled his head and took her mouth.

He brought his fingers up to capture her jaw, lightly, as if she might bolt at any minute. Explored the surface of her mouth with an exquisite thoroughness that just about brought her to her knees. Long and mesmerizing, the kiss went on and on, until she was boneless beneath his fingers, her blood moving through her veins in a hot, restless purr.

He moved his hands to her hips and brought her closer. About as close as their practice kiss. Except this time she didn't feel any fear. She just wanted *more*.

His tongue traced her bottom lip, laving it. Then he nipped gently, taking the sensation to a whole other level. The moan that came from her throat was low, instinctive. He satisfied her demand, dipping his tongue inside her mouth and turning the kiss into a hot, uninhibited exploration.

Her insides contracted. She'd never been kissed like this before. Like he wanted to devour her. *Possess* her. The kisses she'd received from the men she'd dated on her quest to find a husband had been tame. *This was far from tame. It was toe-curlingly sensual, like an overture to an opera, slowly building to the main act.*

She met the bold strokes of his tongue with tentative forays of her own. It was a poor attempt but Nate seemed to like it, stroking her, urging her on with a low husky voice. She grabbed a fistful of his shirt for balance, arching instinctively into him as her body caught fire. His hands shaped her against him, molded her to the hard contours of his powerful body as if he'd been expecting it, waiting for it. She tilted her head back to his demand as he consumed her more deeply.

The thick, powerful evidence of his arousal burned an imprint into her, shocking her, heating the blood in her veins to a whole new level. Her hands curled tighter in his shirt, but she didn't let go. Not when his kiss, when *he*, felt this intoxicatingly good.

Lost in a universe that was all Nate, all about the feel of his hard, hot body against hers, it was a full second or two before she registered the fact that all that heat was gone. That Nate had set her away from him with firm hands that remained on her hips to steady her as her heart pounded near through her chest. As if he knew how completely *unbalanced* she was.

"One kiss," he rasped, his eyes on her face. "And now I'm walking away, Mina. Just like I said I would."

She stared at him. "I—that was—"

"What I hope will erase that other kiss from your memory." His mouth twisted. "Never to happen again."

She nodded. *"Esattamente,"* she agreed shakily. Exactly. Never to be *experienced* again, either, she was fairly sure.

He picked his jacket up off the chair. *"Buonanotte."*

She watched him walk away, as if he regularly brought women to their knees…metaphorically. *Now* she knew why she hadn't accepted any of the suitors her mother had tried to foist on her. Because none of them, not one of the eligible and some of them very good-looking bachelors that had been presented to her, had ever made her feel even one-tenth of what Nate had just done.

Pulling in a deep breath, she kicked off her shoes, picked them up and headed for her bedroom. That might have done the job and knocked everything else clean out of her head. Proved to her she could trust her instincts. The issue, she predicted, was going to be finding a way to think of anything *but* what had just happened.

CHAPTER SEVEN

MINA HAD BEEN RIGHT on her wedding day. A real kiss from Nate *was* unforgettable. She'd spent a sleepless night in her big, soft bed tossing and turning, *imagining* what it would be like to be in his arms. *Wondering* about all the things he would teach her.

Which would stay right there in her imagination, she told herself as she sat in on a marketing meeting with Giorgio and his team to discuss the repeat guests campaign. What Nate had given her was priceless—a chance to prove she was more than just a pretty face whose only opportunities lay in trading on her looks. A chance to prove she was capable of more than providing a graceful introduction at an afternoon tea or cleaning toilets at the Giarruso.

Nate had also given her something perhaps even more important. He'd reminded her last night that despite how overwhelmed she felt in her current situation, she was not simply a creature of God's universe, being batted to and fro by the whims and mercies of the world around her. She was a woman who'd chosen her destiny, who was finally standing on her own two feet.

It was something Celia's mother had taught her on the school holidays she'd spent with the Bettencourts in Nice while her mother jet-setted around the world. When the gaping hole inside of her at never belonging to anything, at being so lonely it ached, had gotten a bit much to take, the certainty she must somehow be defective to never warrant her mother's attention overwhelming the fragile vision of herself she'd built.

"You are special," Juliana Bettencourt had told her. *"You are a bright light, Mina, inside and out. Never forget that. Choose a future for yourself that brings you everything you deserve."*

She was determined to do just that as the marketers around her in the meeting threw about foreign terms like *CRM*—customer relationship management—data and click-through rates. She couldn't blow this opportunity over a kiss, no matter how incredible it had been. Not even if it had made her feel truly alive for the first time in her adult life. Not even if the magnetic, combustible attraction she and Nate shared seemed like the once-in-a-lifetime type.

Over the next few days, she sat in on meetings with Nate about the expansion of the Grand's conventions and meetings program and on a conference call with the global marketing team. On Thursday, they met with the local public relations agency Giorgio and his team used to execute their marketing campaigns. She took the brainstorming ideas they'd generated back to Nate, who added his thoughts, told her they were solid and gave her feedback to take to Giorgio. Having her own project to own and manage put a glow in her cheeks and a spring in her step.

By the time she and Nate stepped on the jet to fly to Hong Kong on Saturday, she was settling nicely into her new role and had lost a bit of her deer-in-the-headlights aura, as Nate liked to describe her as having.

If it hurt that her mother hadn't bothered to call again, the fact that Silvio had also left her alone compensated for it. Apparently he really was done with her.

That worry behind her, all signs pointed straight ahead, no looking back. That's where she was going.

Nate was getting good at this game. He'd spent the last week steadfastly ignoring the explosive chemistry between him and his wife. Putting his protégée through a ruthless schedule of work designed to wipe that kiss from her head.

For the most part, his strategy had worked. Mina had taken everything he'd thrown at her and dedicated herself to producing a thorough, well-thought-out result. The keen insight she'd shown in his suite that day at the Giarruso had proven his instincts about her right. It wouldn't be long before she was an asset to his business.

Where his strategy wasn't so effective, where he and Mina got into trouble, was in the in-between moments, such as this long flight from Capri to Hong Kong via London. Left alone together long enough, the attraction between them began to simmer, find its way through the cracks in their interaction until one of them had to consciously turn it off.

Mina would shoot him one of the sideways glances she'd been directing his way ever since that admittedly hot kiss, her curiosity about what it would be like between them utterly transparent. He, in turn, would deflect those looks with the ruthless efficiency of a man who knew trouble when he saw it.

He'd flicked a switch in his innocent wife's head that night. Awakened her to what true chemistry looked like with a kiss that had gotten a lot more intense than he'd intended. And although he couldn't deny he was curious, too, wouldn't be human if he didn't wonder what peeling back his beautiful wife's layers would reveal, it wasn't going to happen.

Theirs was a marriage of convenience. A business transaction, albeit a slightly more complex one than usual. If that wasn't enough of a deterrent not to take her to bed, the fact that she was a virgin was. He would lay odds of a million to one that his wife was untouched. As such, she was off-limits to him. Virgins were, as a matter of policy, not to be played with.

As Franco had done the night of the Curious party.

A grimace twisted his mouth at the unfinished business he and the actor had. Franco had been like a big cat that night, swiping at Nate's possession with a paw to rile him. The depths to which he had wanted to take him apart for scaring Mina so badly shocked him. It was another reason to stay away from his wife—this intense sense of protectiveness he had toward her. Had had from the beginning.

Mina was too unsullied to exist in his world where relationships were transactional. Where the women in his bed were those who knew their tenure there was temporary. *Exceedingly* temporary. A hot weekend in Rio…a night out at a five-hundred-dollar-a-plate dinner in Manhattan in the name of a good deed…a chance for their name to end up in the society column… It was symbiotic at best. No false expectations; merely the pursuit of mutual pleasure.

Mina was a whole other story. A female of the most dangerous variety, whose innocence and vulnerability demanded everything from a man or nothing at all. He fell into the latter category because creating ties wasn't in his DNA.

He wasn't even willing to invest in his own family. In his half sister Natalia, whose intense vulnerability after she'd been kidnapped and held for ransom while on a gap year in South America had, until recently, kept her housebound. In Dario and Dante, his twin brothers, whose feud had torn the Di Sione family apart. In Matteo, his youngest brother, who had built his wildly successful hedge fund on calculated risks.

Investing in other people simply wasn't part of his portfolio. It came with too much fine print.

Mina, curled up in the seat beside him asleep, stirred, her tousled dark hair and voluptuous curves drawing his eye. It was not a stretch to imagine what she'd look like in his bed as he lavished attention on her from the top of her beautiful head to her equally perfect feet with a long stop in between to idolize the sensational curve of her behind.

The predatory male in him liked the idea of being the first to touch all of that forbidden beauty. The realist knew he could never satisfy the clauses that came with it.

Mina opened her eyes, brown orbs fully alert, as if she'd just been catnapping. He wiped his face clean of his wayward thoughts, but wasn't fast enough. A deep red stain spread across her sleep-flushed cheeks. "What time is it?"

He cursed himself inwardly at the slip. "We have another hour and a half left. I'll brief you on the agenda when you've had a chance to freshen up."

She nodded, rolled to her feet and headed for the bathroom with the haste of a woman who knew what was good for her.

Dio mio. Mina splashed water on her face in the tiny washroom, attempting to wake up her sluggish brain, which seemed to be caught in a time zone somewhere between here and Capri.

She had to stop fantasizing about what it would be like to *be* with her husband. It was never going to happen. Nate had made that clear. But then he went and did something like *that*. Looked at her like he wanted to inhale her, and all their rules went up in flames.

Grabbing a towel, she dried her face and applied a coat of lip gloss to her mouth, her only concession to makeup while traveling. Telling herself sternly to focus, she made her way back into the cabin, pulled a notepad and pen out of her bag and sat down beside Nate.

"We have two goals in Hong Kong." he began. "The first is to meet with a Michelin-starred chef named

Sheng Zhu about a potential in-house restaurant he's proposing for the Grand. It would be a huge coup for the hotel to have him. Mingmei, my manager at the Grand, has been handling the negotiations, but wanted me in attendance to sign the final deal."

Mingmei, his former lover. She ignored the twinge of jealousy that stirred. He had only kissed her to demonstrate a point, for heaven's sake. Nothing more. "Didn't he win one of those top chef shows?"

He nodded. "Unfortunately, he also has a big personality to go with the name. The question is—is he worth the risk? Mingmei thinks he is."

"And the second goal?"

"We'll meet with Mingmei and her team for some general updates on the business this afternoon. Present the global marketing and business plans to the executive team. I'm going to have lunch with a key investor who lives locally to discuss a project. I'll have you take Mingmei through the marketing plan since you know it while I'm tied up. That'll save some time."

By the time Nate finished briefing her and walking her through Sheng Zhu's proposal, they had landed at Hong Kong International Airport. The car Mingmei had sent for them was waiting at the exit, Mingmei herself standing on the sidewalk when the limousine pulled up in front of the red awning of the gold-accented Grand Hotel.

Tall and slim as a wand, the impossibly beautiful Mingmei Gao, as Nate's manager introduced herself, pressed a warm kiss to both Nate's cheeks. Her long, straight jet-black hair, her dark eyes with pencil-thin brows and perfectly shaped red-lipped mouth conspired to make Mina feel a bit lacking in comparison.

The thorough, unabashed appraisal Mingmei gave her cataloged her assets from head to foot. "Welcome to the Grand Hotel Hong Kong," she murmured in impeccable, lightly accented English. "Congratulations on your and Nate's marriage. I hope you'll both be very happy."

If Nate's former lover felt any emotion at all toward her husband, as Susana had hinted was the case, she hid it behind her perfectly composed facade.

"Thank you," Mina replied. "It's been a bit of a... *whirlwind*."

"So much of a whirlwind you haven't taken the time to organize a honeymoon, according to Josephine." Mingmei directed the chiding comment at Nate. "I took the liberty of planning something special for you the night before you leave."

"Special?"

Mingmei's mouth curved. "I have the honeymoon suite for you, of course. The occupants were more than happy to move to the presidential suite."

"That really wasn't necessary."

"Of course it is. Let me show you up."

Another glass elevator, a signature of the Grand, sent them swishing up to the fifty-second floor. Mingmei ushered them into the large, opulent suite, its muted, ambient lighting setting off the luxurious interior done in rich jewel tones. The view of Hong Kong through the floor-to-ceiling windows was breathtaking. But Mina's gaze was fixed on the massive, king-size bed that dominated the adjoining room, rose petals strewn across its ruby-red silk coverlet.

There was only one bed.

Nate turned to Mingmei, a wry look on his face. "You've outdone yourself. Really you didn't need to do this. We can have a regular suite."

Mingmei gave him a pointed look. "You may not be a romantic, but I'm sure Mina appreciates the room."

Mina forced a smile to her frozen face. "*Sì*. It's… amazing. *Mille grazie*."

Mingmei smiled. "I'll leave you to freshen up. I'll meet you in the executive offices at noon, Mina. We can have some lunch and go over the marketing plan."

Mina nodded. Stood staring at the giant, rose petal–covered bed as Nate walked Mingmei to the door.

He had taken a soul-searing possession of her with his kiss that night in Capri. She'd relinquished all common sense, all rational thought. Nate had been the one to call it off. *What was going to happen when they shared a bed together?*

The side of her she was desperately trying to avoid, the newly discovered part of her that clamored to feel more of that sensory overload Nate had evoked in her, knew it for a bad idea. But the desire to experience that kind of passion again—but this time more, *all of it*—was shockingly strong.

"We can't share that bed," she blurted out as Nate walked back into the room.

An amused smile twisted his lips as he came to stand in front of her. "I'm afraid we have no choice."

She glanced around in desperation. "I'll sleep on the floor."

His smile deepened. "No one is sleeping on the floor, Mina. But just for the record, is your adamant proclamation we can't share that bed because you think *you* can't restrain yourself? Because *I* have proven I can be a good boy."

Her jaw dropped. "Do women actually find this… this *arrogance* appealing?"

"Yes," he murmured, bending to bring his mouth to her ear. "You're doing an admirable job of trying to hide your curiosity, Mina, but not quite good enough."

Her heart leaped into her mouth. She stepped back, *away* from all that testosterone. "This is *not* solving our problem."

He nodded toward the bed. "*That* problem I will solve by wearing boxers just for your benefit. Our other problem? We go with avoidance. It's been marginally effective so far."

That Nate ordinarily slept in the nude was disturbing enough to her senses. What he would *look* like in boxers more so.

"You've seen me in a towel," he reminded her. "Same thing. Out of curiosity," he ventured, tilting his head to the side, "what would you have done if the towel had fallen off?"

"Sued you for indecent exposure." Spinning on her heel, she headed for the bathroom. Nate's laughter followed her.

"I wouldn't have been much good as your knight in shining armor sitting in jail now, would I?"

You couldn't think of beds and boxer shorts when you were presenting the global marketing plan to your husband's ex-lover. A respite it would have been if Mina hadn't felt so intimidated in the other woman's presence. Mingmei was as brilliant as she was exquisitely beautiful, asking probing, thoughtful questions about the marketing plan that never would have occurred to Mina. By the time they finished, she felt like a rank amateur.

Her mouth tightening, she clicked out of the presentation and sat back in her chair. "Any further questions?"

Mingmei crossed her arms over her chest. "None of my questions were a criticism, Mina. I wouldn't have expected you to know the answers. They were discussion points to take back to the global team for further thought."

Her chin dipped. She really needed to master that tightly schooled expression her social behavior coaches had failed to conjure up in her.

When Nate texted to say he was running late with his investor lunch, Mingmei's executives had already started to show up for their scheduled meeting. "Why don't you present the marketing plan?" Mingmei suggested. "Nate can do the rest when he comes."

A wave of panic enveloped her. She knew the presentation. But to present it to a team of executives after being on the job for a week? Nate had made it clear she was to stay within her role.

"You want my advice?" Mingmei directed a pointed look at her. "Seize every opportunity you get. If you don't feel comfortable doing something, do it, anyway. Fake the confidence until you have it."

Mina swallowed past the tension climbing her throat. She knew the presentation inside out.

"Si," she said. "I'll do it."

Her knees knocked together as she stood at the front of the conference room, Mingmei introducing her to the half dozen executives who ran the sales, customer service and marketing teams. Her mouth like sawdust, her hands clammy, she clicked the remote to start the presentation. A *gladiator*, she told herself. She was a gladiator.

Her voice tight, her delivery far too rapid, she began. It was a friendly room, thank goodness, with the executives stopping her to ask a question when they wanted to explore a point further. She felt her shoulders and voice loosening as the session turned interactive. By the time Nate walked into the room fifteen minutes later, she was midway through the presentation and firmly in her groove.

His gaze widened, moved from Mina to the table of executives and then back again. She thought he might interrupt and take over. Instead, he pulled up the chair closest to the door and sat down.

Mina kept going, thinking he didn't look angry like he had in the meeting with Giorgio, so maybe she'd made the right choice. Nate watched her from the head of the table, his dark gaze inscrutable as he joined in wherever he was needed, but let her take the reins with the rest.

When she'd finished the presentation, she sat down, her legs like jelly. Her heart was pounding, her head buzzing, an extreme high enveloping her. She hadn't let fear rule her, the fear she wasn't good enough, as it had so many times in her life, and it felt good. *Molto bene.* As if she'd begun to slay her demons.

Nate said nothing until their meetings concluded and they rode the glass elevator skyward to their suite.

"Whose idea was it for you to present?"

"Mingmei suggested I do it." She threw him a sideways look. "Is it okay that I did?"

He nodded. "You did a great job."

She exhaled. "I was worried you'd be angry."

"If you'd gone up there and presented the financial results for the year I would have been, yes. But you presented material you knew." He rested an appraising gaze on her. "I'm thinking of offering you a dual role when we get back to New York. Part of the time as my protégée and part of the time on the global marketing team. *If* you want to go in that direction."

"Sì." She gave a sharp nod of her head. "I do. *Mille grazie.* That means so much to me, Nate."

His mouth quirked. "See what you think when you meet my director of marketing. She's a fire-breathing dragon. But the best in the business."

They joined Mingmei for dinner in the rooftop restaurant with its spectacular view of the city. Watching

Nate's former lover more closely, she determined Susana had been right. Mingmei's repartee with Nate was utterly professional, but every once in a while Mina caught a glimpse of something in the other woman's eyes. *A wistfulness?* An admiration that extended to the man beneath the title.

"Mingmei is lovely," she said as they walked into their suite.

Nate flicked a glance at her. "You should know we were once lovers. In case you hear talk."

She shrugged off her wrap. "Susana told me. I think she thought it was better I knew."

"It was three years ago, before she came to work for me. There is nothing between us now."

On his part. She pressed her lips shut, her gaze dropping away from his. *"You don't have to explain your personal life to me."*

With that, she took her irrational jealousy off to the bathroom to wash up before bed. Nate was still working when she wished him good-night, offering an absent-minded one in return. Determined to be asleep by the time he joined her, she quickly swept the rose petals out of the bed and into the trash can and curled up with a book to put herself to sleep. An hour and a half after she'd gone to bed, she was still awake, staring at the ceiling, when Nate came in.

She averted her gaze as he stripped, hung up his suit and got into bed.

"Can't sleep?"

"No."

"Want me to tell you a bedtime story?"

"No."

Laughter rumbled from his throat. "Likely a good thing. The only ones I can think of would be strictly X-rated."

"Nate!"

"Go to sleep, Mina."

She squeezed her eyes shut. He turned on his side and all was quiet. The clocked ticked loudly on the mantelpiece over the fireplace. *Dannazione*, but she was restless. Rolling on her side she hugged her pillow. It was too soft—she *hated* soft pillows. Reaching for the other pillow she'd dropped on the floor, she tried that one out. It was too hard.

A sigh left her throat.

"Good God." Nate reached over and flicked on the light. Which put his amazing, sculpted chest on display. She'd never *seen* anything like it, muscle and sinew converging in a mouthwatering work of art.

His gaze raked over her face. Dropped lower to the lace nightie Susana had insisted she buy for her honeymoon. The look on his face sent all the blood in her body rushing to her twin heated cheeks.

"I don't sleep much," he said grimly, returning his gaze to her face, "but I do need a few hours. So let me assure you I am not crossing the center line tonight. Despite that enticing scrap of lace you're wearing. Despite the fact that it has *Take me* written all over it and it's not helping by adding to my list of fantasies."

Her gaze tangled with his. His eyes were so dark she could walk right into them and lose herself completely.

It was tempting, so tempting, to do so. To throw common sense out the window.

"Susana made me buy it," she whispered. "Not my idea."

His laser-like stare said that fact was inconsequential.

She turned her back on him, clutching the hard pillow to her, her heart slamming in her chest. She wanted so badly to know what those fantasies were. Wanted his beautiful hands on her as he acted them out. Wanted to feel as alive as he'd made her feel that night in his arms in Capri. To know for once in her lonely life what it was like to be the center of someone's orbit—a man like Nate's orbit. To experience that heady, inescapable passion…

But she wasn't going to be the one to cross the line, either. She had far too much at stake.

CHAPTER EIGHT

THE WEEK IN Hong Kong flew by at a blindingly fast pace. They had an initial meeting with Sheng Zhu the following day in which the celebrity chef outlined his vision for a new avant-garde restaurant at the Grand that, he promised, would be the talk of the city.

Mina got a chance to see the razor-sharp, ruthless side of her new boss as Nate systematically picked Sheng Zhu's proposal apart and pressed for additional exclusivity. She had no doubt he'd walk away from the partnership if it wasn't tailored to his liking, and apparently neither did Sheng Zhu, who promised to return the morning they were to fly out with an updated proposal.

She spent the rest of the week learning the operations of the hotel alongside Nate and Mingmei. By the end of the week her head was so crammed full of information she had almost been able to forget about her and Nate's sleeping arrangements.

Almost. Not that Nate slept. He worked more than any human being she'd ever encountered, coming to bed long after she'd fallen asleep and rising before she did. She had no idea how he functioned with such little rest, but it did the trick, minimizing the contact between them.

Tonight, however, their last night in Hong Kong, was going to be a challenge. Mingmei had prepared a special honeymoon dinner for them in their suite. Unless they wanted to look ungrateful they were going to have to go through the motions.

She eyed the suite warily as she and Nate returned from their meetings. The dining table near the windows with the spectacular view of the harbor had been set for two, tall, tapered candles flickering in the center of it, champagne cooling in an ice bucket. The lighting had been muted, a classic piece by Ella Fitzgerald playing in the background, a tray of oysters at the ready.

Her mouth went dry. Ignoring her attraction to Nate was one thing in a room full of people. Another entirely in the middle of a seduction scene.

A sparkle caught her eye. Moving further into the salon she found an evening gown draped over a chair, a delicate pair of glittering stiletto heels beside it and a card that said *"Wear me"* propped up beside the dress.

Nate strolled over to pick up the embossed envelope that sat beside it.

Sliding the card out, he read its contents. "'A 2002 Piper-Heidsieck is on its way. Enjoy the music and some dancing before your six-course dinner featuring some of Hong Kong's great delicacies.'"

Nate raised an eyebrow at Mina's expression.

"Afraid I'll step on your toes? I happen to be a very good dancer."

He knew exactly what it was she was afraid of and it wasn't the dancing! She tossed her hair over her shoulder in what she hoped was a nonchalant gesture. "I am sure you are very smooth. Part of your lady-killer image."

An openly amused look crossed his face. *"Lady-killer?* Where did you get that from? An old movie?"

She ignored him and picked up the dress. The Asian-inspired design was done in a deep buttercream color with the most exquisite beadwork and embroidery she'd ever seen.

"Go put it on before the champagne comes," said Nate.

She did, if only to distract herself. The dress might have encompassed plenty of material, but it was snug, molded to her body in a perfect fit that emphasized all her curves. The only nod toward daring was the low back that left much of her skin bare.

That Mingmei clearly had a perfect eye for style didn't surprise her in the least. Slipping on the sparkly stilettos, which fit perfectly, she returned to the salon. Nate had taken his jacket off, elegant and minimalistic in a silver-gray shirt and black trousers that molded his muscular body to perfection. His inescapable virility in the suddenly very small space rolled over her in a heady wave of awareness.

His gaze ate her up in a frank appraisal that made her lungs tight. "I should have left my jacket and tie on. In the face of such perfection…"

The breath whished from her lungs. "You're far more relaxed when you're not in a suit and tie."

"I'm not sure relaxed is the state of mind I should be aiming for right now."

Her stomach plummeted. "This...*talk*," she pointed out weakly, "is not helping the situation."

His mouth curved. "I think being self-aware is not a bad thing at the moment."

A discreet cough alerted her to the fact that they were not alone. Turning, she found a black-coated waiter at her elbow, holding a white cloth–wrapped champagne bottle and glasses. Apparently they had their own personal waiter for the evening, a fact that eased her nerves considerably. A chaperone was exactly what she and Nate needed.

The waiter filled their glasses, returned the bottle to the ice bucket and stepped back to stand unobtrusively by the door. Nate set a hand to the small of her back and guided her out onto the terrace with its spectacular views of Victoria Harbor, Hong Kong Island and Kowloon. The press of his strong fingers against the bare skin of her back sent a tremor reverberating through her.

Dannazione. She needed to get a handle on herself.

She focused on the view in front of her. Found herself transfixed by the light exploding over the city. Laser beams and searchlights in a rainbow of hues shot off the tops of the buildings, casting rays of light into the inky sky and harbor. Fireworks dazzled the eye, timed to music she could just make out from this distance. It was a choreographed spectacle the likes of which she'd never seen.

"Fantastico," she breathed. "What's the occasion?"

"It's called the Symphony of Lights. It happens every night. It's meant to celebrate the energy and diversity of Hong Kong."

Mina watched, transfixed. Thought about how spectacular, how *foreign*, it was. She might have been a whole planet away from her home rather than just on another continent.

It struck her then how much her life had changed in two weeks. How exhilarating, terrifying and irrevocable those changes were.

"That's a contemplative look." Nate rested his elbows on the railing and looked over at her.

"This," she said, waving her hand at the view, "feels bittersweet. I wanted it so badly—my freedom. The chance to make my mark. But I also feel...*torn*. Homesick." She sighed. "How silly is that? For a mother who barely tolerates me...a life that made me miserable."

"It's what you know," he said quietly. "Walking into the unknown, even though you know it's the right path, is scary. Sometimes you want to retreat. To stay with the known even though it makes you unhappy."

"Did you feel like that once?"

"More than once." His mouth curved. "I've taken a lot of risks in my life. You don't achieve success without them. But that doesn't mean I've never been afraid—afraid of making the wrong call, afraid the magic will disappear someday just like it appeared. It's human to be afraid. It's what you do with the fear that defines a person."

She found that thought vastly comforting. That Nate,

as successful as he was, had once not been so completely sure of himself.

She took a sip of her champagne. Watched another round of fireworks light up the sky. "I used to lie in bed at school at night after my father died, so scared of the future, of what would happen to me. I'd wonder why God had taken him and not my mother. I used to secretly wish that he *had*, then be terrified he'd punish me for thinking such awful thoughts."

"I would say that's understandable thinking coming from an eight-year-old."

"Perhaps." She lifted a shoulder. "To me they seemed wicked and irredeemable thoughts. So I made up a pretend family instead to keep me company. I had five brothers and sisters so I'd never be lonely, a dog named Gigi, who slept on the end of my bed, and parents who came to get me for every holiday."

He frowned. "Your mother left you alone for some of them?"

"Often. After I met my friend Celia, I would spend the holidays with her family."

He was silent for a long moment. "You'll have a family of your own someday," he said finally.

Would she? Did she crave the fantasy more than the reality? She had so much she wanted to accomplish before then, most of all finding out *who* she really was. *What* she wanted.

"Who was your mentor?" she asked Nate. "The one you spoke of?"

"My grandfather, Giovanni. He put me through university, took me in to work at Di Sione Shipping with him."

"Is this the same grandfather who wants the ring?"

"Yes."

"You said before your father wasn't a part of your life. How did you come to know your grandfather?"

"My father died in a car accident when I was ten. My relationship with Giovanni began in my late teens when he developed leukemia and needed a bone marrow transplant. None of my half siblings were a match, so my eldest brother, Alex, sought me out to see if I was. I was a match and I did the transplant. Our relationship developed from there."

Wow. "That must have been an incredibly emotional introduction to each other."

"It was…intense."

"You said you weren't close to your brothers and sisters?"

He took a sip of his champagne. Rested his glass on the railing, a distant look in his eyes. "There is too much history between us to make that possible."

"How so?"

"A lot of complicated relationships with many layers. Sometimes it's simply easier to leave the past in the past. To not reopen old wounds."

She recalled the lack of a personal background in his media profiles. It had not been an accident. He was protecting a past he had distanced himself from.

What had driven his father to abandon him? What had happened to keep him and his siblings from becoming close after his father's death when one would think it would have been the ultimate bonding experience to give his grandfather his life back?

It was an incredibly enticing train of thought to want to pursue, but she left it at that because the walls around him as he stared out into the night said that particular conversation was over.

"Giovanni is very lucky to have had you."

The lazy, seductive bars of a Duke Ellington tune filled the silence that followed. "I think it's the other way around," he said finally. "But I won't have him for much longer. His leukemia is back and this time it will kill him."

Her stomach dropped. That was why his grandfather wanted the ring. To reclaim a piece of his past before it was all lost to him.

"Nate—" She put a hand on his arm. "*Mi dispiace.* I'm so sorry."

His expression hardened. "It's fine. I'm lucky to have had him as long as I have."

Except it wasn't fine. She could see just how *un*fine it was in the glitter of emotion that darkened his eyes. In the clench of his jaw. The way his gaze refused to meet hers. He was suffering but you would never have known it. Taking a precious memory back to his mentor, who had perhaps been the father figure he'd never known, only to watch him die.

"It's okay," she said quietly, "for it not to be fine."

He spared her a glance. "What else can it be? He's dying and there's nothing I nor anyone can do to prevent it."

"Talking about it might help."

"I've come to terms with it." Storm clouds gathered in his eyes. "Leave it alone, Mina."

She did. The pieces of her enigmatic husband starting to fall into place, she finished her champagne in silence. So much loss, so much pain, and no way to express it because he considered himself the ultimate gladiator. He would never show weakness.

A Frank Sinatra tune she loved drifted out to them on the night air. Nate put his glass down and held out his hand. "So we can say we danced at least one song after all the trouble Mingmei went through."

She thought maybe that was a bad idea. The champagne was starting to hit her bloodstream, infusing her with that languorous, dangerous desire to play with fire. Not a good idea when keeping things on a business level between her and Nate seemed so very important.

He pulled her close. Close enough that she felt his hard thighs brushing against hers, the intoxicating, spicy smell of him filling her senses. His big hand was laced through hers, while the other rested lightly on her waist as he guided her expertly through the steps.

He hadn't been lying about being a good dancer. He was rather dreamy, in fact. She'd danced with a great deal of men at all the social events she'd endured, but somehow dancing under the stars with Nate with only Sinatra to accompany them was an experience of an entirely different realm.

He was so strong, so heart-poundingly virile, it was impossible not to think how easily he could command her if he wanted to. To do all sorts of *unthinkable* things. Her thoughts should have put her guard up. Instead, she was afraid of what he might *never* do to her. What might never happen between them.

"She's in love with you, you know."

"Who?"

"Mingmei. She didn't say it, but I can see it."

An impassive expression claimed his face. "We ended things on good terms. Mingmei knew the deal with me."

The question that had been burning a hole in her head all week tumbled from her lips. "Why? Why break things off with her? Mingmei is stunning, intelligent, extroverted, *entertaining*... How could she possibly be lacking in any department?"

"It isn't about how amazing a woman is or isn't. I'm not interested in a permanent relationship with anyone."

"Don't you ever get lonely?"

His lips curved in a cynical twist. "I don't mean sex," she qualified, blushing. "I mean for true companionship."

"And how would you define true companionship sweet, innocent Mina?" He swung her into a tight circle, his gaze holding hers. "Having *sleepovers* with the women I date so I can spill my deepest, darkest secrets to them? Telling her how I *feel* over breakfast so I can start the day a *whole* man?"

Her chin lifted. "I mean someone who's there at the end of the day to confide in, whether you've had the best day or the worst. Someone who *cares* what your day is like. Who nurtures the emotional side of you."

"I don't *have* an emotional side."

Not one he would admit. Pretending he didn't care was his self-defense mechanism as much as hers had been withdrawing into herself for so many years. Because she had *seen* him care. Everything he had done for her had been about caring for her welfare. It was more than just paying it forward.

"Everyone needs human connection, Nate. I told myself I didn't need it. I spent my whole life without it, but nothing can replace what the unconditional love of someone gives us. We *need* emotional connection to survive."

"Some of us do. And some of us exist better as solitary beings." His mouth curled. "Get married and have your white picket family, Mina. All the power to you. But that's not me."

"Who says I want to settle down now? I want my freedom now that I have it. The rest can come later."

"You *think* you want your freedom. Soon you'll want more. All women have the nesting gene."

His condescending attitude irked her. "I guess that's right if you say so."

His gaze sharpened. "Picking a fight, Mina? That's a new one."

"Maybe I'm tired of being told what I want. There's a whole world out there for me to experience, Nate. Not just business. I plan on doing so."

His steps slowed as another, lazier, Sinatra tune followed the last. "I'm all for seizing the moment," he murmured idly. But the gaze he had trained on her was anything but. "So what will you do when our year is up, then? Take a series of lovers to satisfy your need for *human connection*? Keep your affairs short and sweet so no one gets too attached?"

"You're playing with me now."

"I'm *curious*. You forget I know you're an innocent, Mina. How does that factor into all this? Do you plan to simply give your virginity away to the first man who *does* it for you?"

Her lashes lowered. *If that were the case, she'd be giving it to him.*

"My virginity is a matter of circumstance. A bargaining tool my mother used to *sell* me. I refuse to treat it as such. When I decide to give it to a man it will be because I made a conscious decision to do so without overcomplicating things."

"I *see*." He nodded thoughtfully. "That's quite a thing to lay at a man's doorstep. What happens if he falls for you? You simply kick him out the door and say you're not ready?"

She frowned. "Who says it would be me kicking him out?"

"Because you are devastatingly, undeniably desirable, Mina. With just the right air of vulnerability to have men falling over themselves to claim you if you offer them your innocence. They won't stand a chance."

Her gaze locked with his for a long, heated moment. It seemed ridiculous to be speaking of other lovers when the only man's hands she wanted on her were Nate's. When that's all she'd wanted ever since he'd unleashed that devastating kiss on her.

"Not happening, Mina." His husky drawl slid over her sensitized flesh like a slow, potent caress. "*We* have a very functional partnership going on here."

She knew it. He knew it. But she couldn't seem to tear her gaze away from his. "I know," she agreed. "I know it's insanity, but I—I can't seem to stop thinking about what happened between us. About how alive... how *lost* I felt."

"Try harder," he bit out. "*This, we,* cannot happen. I don't mix business with pleasure."

"You're the one who said we hardly have a straight-forward business relationship. I believe you called it... *unique.*"

"Unique enough," he growled. The storm in his eyes intensified. "You are vulnerable, Mina. You are look-ing at me like I'm some knight who's come to your res-cue when I am anything but. You have no idea what you are throwing out there right now."

She swallowed hard. "I *am* vulnerable right now but I *want* to feel vulnerable. I *want* to want what I want. I want to figure out who I am. And I am under no il-lusions as to what this would be between us. I've just said I'm not looking for a commitment. Not now. Not for a long while."

He was silent, so heart-stoppingly silent she could hear her heart pounding in her ears. "Just to be clear," he rasped finally, "you're telling me you want us to go to bed together. And to hell with the consequences?"

She bit the inside of her mouth. *Hard.* "You keep baiting me, Nate. You won't leave it alone, either. What do *you* want?"

* * *

She had a point, Nate thought blackly. *What did he want?* Because he couldn't seem to leave this thing with Mina alone. Not when she felt this good in his arms. When the floral, delicate smell of her, the soft curves that tempted him beyond reason, were his for the taking.

He had gone on the offensive to try and distract her when she'd started prying into the pieces of his life he would never expose. In doing so, he'd started something he couldn't finish. *Definitely couldn't finish.* Proving that seemed to be the way to go.

He let go of her hand. Reached up to trace a line down the silky-soft skin of her cheek to her mouth, his thumb dragging across the plump skin of her lower lip. "What you should be afraid of," he drawled, "is me taking you up on your offer, Mina, because even I have my limits and I'm fast approaching them, common sense be damned."

Her eyes widened. But she drifted closer, not further away as he explored her lips with the rough pad of his fingertip.

"Mina," he growled. "You should walk away. I'm not your human connection project. I promise you that."

She stayed where she was, her gaze fixed on his. He sank his thumb into the warmth of her mouth. Watched the heat in her beautiful dark eyes catch fire. And lost his mind just that much more.

His hands dropped to her hips, tugging her forward until her delectable curves were pressed against him.

Mina's long, silky lashes arced over her cheeks as he angled his head and brought his mouth down on hers.

Urgently, deliberately, he drank her sweetness in, tasted her endlessly until there was not one millimeter of her lips he hadn't explored. When her hand curled around the back of his neck and urged him closer, he teased her mouth further apart and invaded with his tongue. She had learned from the last time they'd kissed, found her rhythm quickly now, her tongue sliding delicately against his. His body hardened in an instant visceral response that should have stopped him. Instead, it spurred him on.

The bare skin exposed by the back of her dress was an irresistible temptation. He swept his palm from her shoulder blades to the base of her spine, urging her closer. Her shocked gasp as she came into contact with his aroused, pulsing body heated his blood.

"There's still time to run," he murmured, dragging his mouth across her cheek and up to her earlobe.

She did the opposite, arching into him, fitting herself to him so perfectly it tore a groan from his throat. Holding her with the fingers he had pressed against the small of her back, he held himself completely still. "You make me crazy," he muttered, wrapping his lips around the tender flesh of her lobe and nipping at it. "Move, Mina. *Now*."

She tipped her head back and gave him more room to explore. He took her lobe deeper into the heat of his mouth and scraped his teeth across it.

"Nate..." she breathed in that way of hers that made it sound more like *Neet*.

Crazy sexy.

He worked his way down the column of her throat to the place where her pulse raged at the base of her neck. Pressed hot, openmouthed kisses against the delicate flesh he found there. Mina shuddered. Wrapped her fingers in his hair.

He brought his mouth back up to hers and took her lips in a hard, hot kiss. Unable to resist, he cupped one of her perfect, uptilted breasts in his palm. She stiffened as he ran his thumb over its delicate, half-erect peak. Over and over again until she moaned and melted into him.

"You like that?" he murmured against her lips, transferring his attention to her other rounded globe.

"Sì," she whispered. "I feel like I'm on fire, Nate."

His head exploded. Dissolved into urgent flames that obliterated any last vestiges of common sense. Rasping his thumb across her nipple, he teased it into a hard, urgent pebble that matched its twin.

Mina moved insistently, urgently, against him now. He cupped her derriere, that part of her he'd been wild for from the beginning, and adjusted the fit so she had him between the V of her thighs. Taut and perfectly shaped, she fit the palms of his hands so well he knew that would be how he'd take her. *If* he took her, which of course he wouldn't.

Their first course was coming any minute. Time was running out.

Mina moved against the solid column of his flesh, rubbed against him like a cat scratching an itch. *"Sì,* just like that. Nate—*per favore—"*

Mother of God. She was so far gone.

He backed her up against the wall. Sliding his hands up the backs of her legs, he brought her dress up with them. Relief was all he was giving her. Then he was ending this insanity.

Her gasp as he cupped the warmth between her thighs was so intoxicating he almost lost it right there. Tightening his fingers, he moved them against her in a slow rock that had her hips thrusting against his hand. *Dear Lord, but she was responsive.*

Moving his hand back up the flat plane of her stomach, he sank his fingers beneath the waistband of her panties and found her hot, velvet warmth. She felt like heaven. *So aroused, wet for him.* It made the blood in his head pound against his temples.

"Spread your legs, baby," he whispered in her ear. "I need room."

She moved her thighs apart for him, her legs trembling so much he had to hold her up with one hand while he brought the thumb of his other to the tight bundle of nerves at the heart of her. Slowly, languorously, he rotated his thumb against her. Italian words tumbled out of Mina's mouth, husky, unbearably sexy. Her hands gripped the concrete behind her, her eyes closed.

He bent and took her mouth with his own, swallowing every cry, every moan, as he stroked her wet heat. She writhed as he moved his thumb against her clitoris in an erratic movement that prolonged her pleasure, kept her orgasm just out of reach. Mina arched her back and sunk her teeth into that delectable bottom lip. Her breathing grew fractured, desperate. *"Per favore.* More."

He gave it to her, sinking two of his long fingers inside her tight, wet heat. Slowly at first, he entered her, giving her a chance to get used to him. Then he picked the rhythm up, plunging deep inside of her.

Her cries came fast and urgent against his mouth. "Nate…"

Neet.

Gritting his teeth against the surge of lust that knocked him sideways, he found her core with his thumb and made her come in a deliberate series of movements that pushed her over the edge. Long and hard, the orgasm shook her petite frame. He caught her against him as her knees gave way and held her through every last shudder of it.

Never had a woman's release turned him on more. Never had it made him shake with the need to have her.

It brought him hurtling back to vivid, mind-altering reality. *To what he had done.*

He told himself he hadn't taken her. That he could still bring this back under control…

It was a lie he couldn't force himself to swallow. *Hadn't crossed a line? He'd just crossed the Great Divide.* He had wanted to touch Mina. He had goaded himself and her into it, to the point of no return, and then he'd walked across the line.

The sound of dishes rattling came from inside the suite. *Their first course.*

He set Mina away from him with unsteady hands, his head too full of emotion for the first time in his life to make sense of what had just happened. To process any of it. He could no more eat dinner right now than he could look at the stripped-down, dazed look on his wife's face. *His wife's face. Dear Lord.*

"I need to go."

"What?" Mina pushed her dress down around her hips. "Dinner is here."

He raked a hand through his hair. "Eat without me."

Her face crumpled. "Nate—"

He turned on his heel and left.

CHAPTER NINE

"SHOULD WE MOVE ON to the timeline?" Sheng Zhu prompted.

Nate nodded. He'd heard enough during the first ten minutes of the celebrity chef's presentation to know it was a partnership the Grand would sign on to. Sheng Zhu was offering the five-year exclusivity he'd demanded, the numbers looked sound and it was clear the chef was a smart businessman first, hotheaded personality second. He'd given them everything they'd wanted.

Unfortunately, the significant part of a bottle of his favorite single-malt Scotch, consumed in a swank watering hole called the American Bar last night, hadn't solved his other problem. All it had done was give him a throbbing headache and no answers about what to do with his sexy, irresistible wife.

He sat back in his chair and brought his steaming cup of coffee with him, wincing as his head protested the movement. Mingmei threw him one of those curious glances she'd been sending his way, as if her spies had told her he'd walked out on his and Mina's dinner. Or maybe it was just because he'd tuned out half an hour ago.

He'd been a fool to think he could ever control this thing between him and Mina. Their chemistry was too strong, the opportunities to exploit it too plentiful. He'd like to say he could turn back the clock and wipe out that brief moment of insanity last night, but it wasn't going to happen. Not when the awareness between him and Mina pulsed across the table like a living, breathing entity. Not when he'd put his hands on her in the most intimate way possible and made her cry out his name with the lights of Hong Kong blazing around them.

Mina gave him a veiled look from beneath her lashes. *Confusion, hurt, apprehension.* He hadn't come back to their suite until well past midnight last night, the six-course dinner long cleared away. Had gone to the gym early this morning to keep some distance between them.

He cared about her. Genuinely cared about her, which was a first for a woman. But he could never offer Mina what she would eventually want—that white picket fence and a family to banish the loneliness she'd carried with her for so long.

She claimed she could handle an affair between them, but could she really? Would it turn their working relationship into an awkward, untenable partnership that worked for neither of them when it was over? Could she give him her virginity in the uncomplicated transaction she'd spoken of and walk away after this year without emotional ties?

If he didn't take her up on the offer, then someone else would. He closed his eyes as the image of a man like Franco becoming Mina's first lover made his head throb.

He took a long sip of his coffee. He could shut it down between them. Fall back on his excuse he never mixed business with pleasure, but Mina was right. Their relationship had already blurred so many lines, there was no going back. The only question was how to move forward.

Mina stood and forced a smile to her face as they concluded their meeting with Sheng Zhu, exchanging bows all around. It had been easy to keep to her role of active listener today. Her brain was running in circles, like a dog chasing its tail, humiliation and confusion taking turns preserving the momentum.

Why had Nate walked out on her like that? What had she done wrong? Why had he looked so angry?

She didn't regret one second of what had happened between them. Learning to go after what she wanted in life, enjoying these heady initial successes, had stoked her craving to experience everything life had to offer. But, she acknowledged miserably, if it was going to ruin everything she and Nate had started to build together, then it had been a big mistake.

Which it might just have been. She had fallen asleep at midnight with Nate still not back, the sumptuous dinner Mingmei had arranged for them sent back virtually untouched. Then woken up to his stone-cold, unapproachable face this morning when he'd come back from the gym.

Had she pushed him too far? He had been pushing, too. Challenging her. Tempting her. It had not been a one-way street.

Swallowing the lump in her throat, she headed for the coffee machine before their next meeting. Nearly jumped out of her skin when a shadow fell over her.

"A word, please."

Nate's sophisticated cologne filled her head in a tantalizing reminder of last night. She risked a look up at him. He still looked distinctly *agitated*.

He jerked his head toward the hallway. She followed him, the snap of the door as it shut behind them making her flinch.

He turned and rested a hand against the wall. "We need to talk."

Sì. They did. Before she crawled right out of her skin.

"I think it should wait until we get to the Maldives," he said tersely. "I have a pile of work to do on the flight. And this particular conversation needs to be done in private."

She couldn't read anything from his expression. *Nothing.*

"I agree."

But it wasn't so easy to endure an entire morning of meetings before they boarded the jet for the Maldives. Nor the several-hour flight in a strained silence between them. By the time they set down on the short, single runway in the tiny island republic in the middle of the Indian Ocean, she *had* crawled out of her skin.

A car took them to the harbor, where a boat transported them the rest of the way to the exclusive resort Nate was about to buy, situated on its own private island. Mina's breath caught as the boat pulled up alongside a dock with a private villa attached to it. Perched in the middle of the ocean with only a narrow walkway connecting it to the island and resort, it was a floating paradise.

Lights glittered inside the grass-roofed villa as sunset approached, illuminating its luxurious interior. A private plunge pool, Jacuzzi and lounge area completed the idyllic picture. But all Mina could look at was the endless vista of blue all around them, as if they were alone in the middle of the ocean.

This was where they were staying? It seemed far too intimate, far too inescapable, no matter which way their conversation went.

A white-shirted butler emerged from the villa, introduced himself and spirited their luggage inside. Nate went with him. Mina stayed outside drinking in the view. They had beautiful beaches in Sicily, but they were crowded and busy and this…this was like nothing she'd ever experienced before.

Nate appeared beside her, his jacket and tie gone, the top buttons of his shirt undone. "I thought we could have a drink and enjoy the sunset before dinner."

Her pulse kicked up, her palms growing damp. She nodded and swallowed back her nerves. "I'd like to change first."

He inclined his head toward the villa. "I'll see what there is to choose from."

She found her luggage in the airy, dark-paneled bedroom with its king-size bed, perfectly positioned to enjoy the sunset and sunrise from through the tall, sliding glass doors that fronted the villa.

One bed. Was it an indication of where Nate's thoughts lay? Or what had been appointed to them? Rather than cater to the nerves consuming her, she exchanged her pants and shirt for a white floral printed dress and rejoined Nate on the terrace.

He was standing, his gaze on the horizon as the sun sank below it, a fiery ball of flame on a canvas of turquoise blue. She padded across the warm wood in her bare feet to his side.

"It's almost unreal, isn't it?"

He nodded. "Perhaps unfair only a select few ever get to experience it."

"The deal is almost done, you said?"

"We should finalize it this week if all the requested enhancements have been made to the property."

And then they would head home to New York. *Her* home now. The thought of being immersed in Nate's world, taking her place as his wife with so much tension between them, made her stomach tighten.

He plucked a bottle of wine from the ice bucket and poured them both a glass of the rosé. She eyed the glass he handed her warily, a flush filling her cheeks. "I'm not sure I should have any of that."

His gaze rested on her with disturbing precision. "The way you responded to me last night was beautifully uninhibited, Mina. A massive turn-on for a man. It's not something to be ashamed of."

Then why had he walked away?

He set a palm to the small of her back and directed her toward the lounge area. She sat down on the sofa beside him, curling her bare legs beneath her as a breeze sent a delicious waft of air over her heated skin.

Nate took a sip of his wine, then cradled the glass against his chest, his gaze resting on her. "I needed to give us both time to think last night. To slow things down so we use our heads and not our hormones to decide if us having an intimate relationship is a good idea."

Her breath snagged in her throat. *So he was considering it.* She set her wine on the coffee table. "You think I didn't mean what I said. That because I have no experience, I can't handle a relationship with you."

"Can you? Can we layer the complexity of a sexual relationship onto what we already have and expect it to be manageable for both of us? Because if we can't, if we don't walk into this with the same expectations, we need to shut this down. *Now.* My primary concern is ensuring you flourish, Mina, so you build a career for yourself and you can stand on your own two feet when this is over. You've gone through too much for me not to do that."

She nodded. "You've set me on that course. You know how much I appreciate it. But nothing is going to distract me from it. It means too much to me."

He gave her a long look, his dark gaze contemplative. "I'm not sure you can separate your vision of me as hero with the reality of who I am. *What* I am."

That may be true, but she wasn't sure that was possible in any aspect of their relationship. What they were was unique because of the way it had started. That was never going to change. But what happened next was about them both making adult decisions fully conscious of what they were doing. And she knew what she was doing.

She took a sip of wine to bolster her courage. "I want you to be my first lover, Nate. I want to experience that with you. I want it to be as memorable as I know it can be. I don't expect anything more of you and I won't let it affect our working relationship."

His gaze widened imperceptibly. "I'm not sure you can make that assurance."

"I can and I will."

He turned his gaze to the horizon. Silence fell between them, the cry of the birds flying overhead the only sound to break it. "Maybe I should ask the same of you," she ventured quietly. "What do you want of me, Nate?"

He looked back at her, the glitter in his eyes sending her heart into a free fall. "I want what I've wanted from the beginning. You in my bed, Mina. To explore every perfect inch of you with my mouth and my hands and everything else at my disposal."

She sucked in a breath. They were surrounded by hazy, purple sky, but it didn't seem to be supplying enough oxygen to her brain to fix her spinning head.

Wine seemed to be the answer. The sparkling rosé

was delicious: tart and refreshing. It slid down easily as the sun sank into the sea, leaving behind it a stunning dusky-pink-stained sky. By the time she'd finished it, she'd almost convinced herself it was doing the trick—relaxing her taut limbs and clearing her head. Then Nate set his hand over hers, laced their fingers together and her pulse flatlined.

She looked down at his strong, elegant hand. Thought about what he'd done to her with it last night and her stomach did a slow roll.

"You want dinner?" he asked quietly.

She lifted her gaze to his and shook her head.

A purposeful heat blazed to life in his eyes. He took the empty glass from her hand and set it on the coffee table. His hands settled around her waist to lift her up and bring her down on his lap so her knees straddled his thighs.

Her breath caught in her throat. *Dio mio.* He was all hard muscle beneath her, the intensity of his dark gaze fixed on hers. She might have been tempted to run if the want in his eyes hadn't drawn her in and kept her right where she was.

"You are so very beautiful," he said huskily. "You do something to me, Mina. I forget my common sense. I forget everything but having you."

She wasn't sure if that was a compliment or a criticism. She didn't much care when he lowered his head and took her mouth in one of those teasing, devastating kisses that rendered her brain useless. Her hands settled on his jaw, her mouth seeking his. Back and forth they exchanged the initiative, kissing and being kissed. Exploring and being explored. Slow, lazy kisses that seemed to match the night darkening around them, pulling them further and further under each other's spell.

Lips, tongue, sexy little nibbles. They did it all, for ages, until she wondered if Nate would do anything *else*.

She gave his lip a frustrated tug with her teeth. Nate pulled back, an amused glint in his eyes. "What was that for?"

"Aren't you going to—I mean—*you know…*?"

He reclined back against the seat, his mouth curving. "I'm right here, Mina. Yours for the taking."

Her insides twisted at the invitation. But his mouth was soft from their kisses, his eyes a molten dark brown. He was letting her take the lead, making sure she was comfortable. Putting her first as he always did. She swallowed, her chest tight.

Pulling her gaze from his hot, watchful study, she worked the top button of his shirt free, then painstakingly worked her way down the row. Her throat went dry as she exposed more and more of his beautiful torso. Flat, hard and defined, he was incredible. His swift intake of air when her fingers brushed against his lower abs was headily empowering.

The last button undone, she found her next move surprisingly intuitive. Splaying her palms across his hot, hard skin, she bent her head and pressed her lips to the sinewy solid muscle, absorbing his earthy, salty flavor. Nate made a sound of approval low in his throat, his hands falling to the sofa to give her better access.

Pulling back, she moved her fingertips down over his pectoral muscles to the hard points that were so much alike, yet so very different from hers. Nate sucked in a breath. "Careful. Men are very sensitive there."

She traced him gently. Moved her thumbs back and forth over him. He let her play for a few moments, then grabbed her hands and dragged them down to her sides. "Enough of that."

She wondered where to go next, but she needn't have worried. Nate took control, pressing a hot kiss to the sensitive skin at the base of her neck as he swept the straps of her dress off her shoulders. His mouth followed his hands as he eased the material away from her skin, his lips finding the soft flesh of her upper breasts, the hollow in between. She held her breath as he pushed the material lower and bared her breasts to his gaze. The lust in his eyes as he palmed her flesh made her stomach curl. "So beautiful."

She closed her eyes. The brush of his thumbs across her nipples in a slow sweep made her gasp. The sensation of his touch on her bare skin was even better than last night. So much more intense...

A wet heat enveloped one of the peaks. Her eyes flew open. Nate's dark head was bent to her, his mouth closed around her aching flesh. She squeezed her eyes shut as he laved her with his tongue, scraped at her with his teeth, sucked on her. A low moan escaped her throat.

"You like that?" he asked. Mina's head tipped up and down. He lavished the same treatment on its twin until her fingers were in his hair holding on for dear life and her whole body felt tense and on edge.

"Nate," she begged. "It's too much."

He lifted his head. Settled her further back on his thighs. The sweep of his hot palms up her inner thighs, squeezing her flesh as he went, was tantalizing, blindingly intimate. "You don't need less," he murmured. "You need different."

She remembered *different* from last night. She wanted more of it. Except it was too intimate, him watching her face as he moved closer to the heat between her legs. Her eyes drifted closed. *Waiting, anticipating.*

His hands stilled. "Open your eyes. I want to see what I do to you."

Her breath left her in a whoosh. *"No."*

"Yes."

She opened her eyes. He swept the filmy material of her panties aside and slid his fingers against her hot, wet flesh. Her lashes fluttered closed as a bolt of heat went through her. *She couldn't do it.*

His wicked fingers played over her, slid inside her. She arched against them, urged him on. Nate's breath was hot at her ear, telling her how much he loved how she responded to him, how sexy she was. As wicked as his hands were, his raspy voice was sexier, unearthing a heated flush all over her body. *Hot*, she was far too hot to breathe.

"Nate," she gasped.

His ebony gaze scorched hers. "Baby, the way you say my name…it makes me crazy."

His hands slid away from her. She started to protest, her body screaming for relief. He lifted her off him and set her on the sofa, dropping to his knees in front of her.

"Nate—"

"Relax," he murmured. "I'm not finished."

She gaped at him. "What are you—Nate, you can't do that."

He nudged her legs apart and moved between them. "You'll like it, I promise."

"Yes, but—"

He slid the hem of her dress unerringly up her thighs. "But what?"

"It's *shocking*."

"Shocking," he agreed, sliding his hands under her buttocks to pull her to the edge of the sofa.

Oh, mio Dio. Her head fell back against the cushions as his hands swept the lacy underwear off her and tossed them to the side. Her eyes closed, her heart slamming in her chest as his palms pushed her thighs apart and his fingers parted her most intimate flesh. A long, slow lap of his tongue brought her hips off the sofa. "Nate—" she breathed. He set a hand to her stomach to ground her, held her in place while he consumed her, every stroke against her hot, moist flesh taking her past her initial sensitivity into a deeper, headier pleasure.

Again and again he stroked her until she was begging, saying his name in a broken tone. Voicing his husky approval, he brought his fingers back into play, easing them inside of her. The penetration along with his hot, amazing mouth on her drove her higher, past where she'd been last night. Until she could take it no more.

"*Per favore.* Please—"

He closed his mouth over her clitoris and sent her tumbling into another universe.

She was still coming down from her orgasm when Nate scooped her up and carried her into the dark, silent bedroom. She stood, knees shaking, legs ready to give way, as he flicked on a light and cast the room in a soft glow.

The lust on his face as he wrapped a hand around her waist and drew her back to him made her even weaker. "Okay?"

She nodded.

A smile tipped his lips. "That wasn't too improper?"

"*Sì*, it was. But I liked it."

The fire in his eyes made her insides dissolve into a throbbing pool of heat. He tipped her chin up with his finger and pressed a lingering kiss against her mouth. She stood on tiptoe, wound her arms around his neck and kissed him back. Pressed against him in search of closer contact. Froze as she felt his rock-hard erection throb against her belly.

Goodness, but he was big. *Was that normal?* How would she handle him?

She stepped back. Pulled in a deep breath. Nate frowned, looking more than a little hot and bothered. "What?"

"*That.*" Her gaze dropped to the bulge in his pants. "I—should I be doing something about that for you now? The girls in school said—"

"Said what?"

"That a woman could—you know—take the edge off for a man."

His mouth twitched. She had the awful feeling he was laughing at her. "It's true," he said solemnly. "Men do enjoy that. I'd prefer to take the edge off *with* you, however."

Her insides did a slow twist. "*Sì.* That's fine, then."

Nate turned her around. Set his lips to her nape. "It will be more than fine."

She quivered under his kiss as he slid the zipper of her dress down to her waist. He pushed it off her shoulders and let it slide to the floor. Air wafted across her shoulders in a delicate caress. He pressed a kiss to her shoulder blades, sank to his knees and continued his kisses, lingering at the indentation at the small of her back. Then his mouth was on the curve of her bottom.

She pulled in a breath. "Nate. What *are* you doing?"

"Indulging myself," he said huskily, his mouth against her skin. "I've had fantasies about this particular part of your anatomy."

Oh. Hands on her hips, he turned her around. His dark gaze was hot on her body. Far too intense to take. "Stunning," he said quietly. "You are every man's dream."

She stared at him, unable to look away. She didn't care if she was anyone else's dream. She only wanted to be his.

His hands tightened around her hips, drawing her to him. Mina watched as his eyes zeroed in on the dark curls between her legs. "No," she said, grabbing a handful of his hair. "Nate—no—"

He put his mouth to her. Stirred her back to life with every reverent kiss. Her body tightened. Thought ceased. By the time he rose to his feet, lifted her into his arms and deposited her on the bed, she was panting for him.

He stripped off his shirt, then the rest of his clothing. Mina's eyes grew wide. *How was this going to work? It* couldn't *work.*

He came down on the bed beside her. Brought his mouth to hers. "You were made to take me," he murmured against her lips. "I promise you, Mina. Trust me."

She did. Her mouth softened beneath his, her body slackening under his caresses. His hands left her to roll a condom on, his jerky, quick movements telling her how much he wanted her. Then he was between her legs, sliding her knees further apart and moving his hand beneath her bottom to cup her buttock. Palming himself, he lifted her and brought his huge shaft to her core. Mina closed her eyes and waited for the pain. Nate played with her instead, getting her used to the feel and pressure of him.

When she could take it no longer, she arched her hips. "Nate. *Per favore.*"

His ebony eyes flashed in the dim light. "You want me, baby?"

"Sì."

He sank into her just enough to stretch her body. Waited while she accommodated him. When she raised her hips for more, he gave it to her, watching her face the entire time, making it such an intensely erotic experience she forgot her fear.

She arched her hips again, took more of him in until she felt a pressure, a resistance. "A little bit of pain and then lots of pleasure," he promised huskily. She nodded and grabbed a handful of sheet as he surged forward and broke through the barrier. A searing pain lanced through her. She breathed through it, Nate holding himself completely still. Then the pain was fading and she felt only full, stretched by his virility. *Possessed*.

"Okay?" His dark eyes were glazed with the effort it was taking him to hold back.

She nodded. Forced her limbs to relax as he started to move, ever so slowly as her body softened around him. Discomfort turned to pleasure as he stroked every nerve ending inside of her, filling her, then withdrawing. Her hips started to move, demanding more. Nate's gaze burned into hers. "Good?"

"*Sì*. So good, Nate. I had no idea it could be so… *good*."

"I told you," he said, taking both her buttocks in his hands now as he brought his mouth down on hers, "your beautiful body was made for me."

His words did something to her insides. Dissolved her into a pool of lust as he stroked deeper. But it was more than that. He might not see the connection between them but she did. It was special. *Powerful*.

She arched her hips and took him deeper. Begged for more against his mouth. He made her say his name as she begged, filling her deeper, harder. Again and again until she was burning up. His hand at her buttock angled her, then as he moved even deeper, touched a place inside of her that promised pleasure like none before. She bit into his lip to urge him on. Nate growled and surged harder inside of her. "I need you with me, baby. Can you feel that?"

"*Sì*. Oh, Nate."

He drove into her then, the animalistic, desperate pace he set stirring her blood to a fever pitch. She matched him stroke for stroke until he hit that spot inside of her and tore her apart, her orgasm so intense she buried her fingernails in his thighs.

His big body tensed, then shuddered against her, his hands clamping hard around her buttocks. When he was finally still, he rolled over on his back and brought her down on his chest. Slowly her world righted itself.

She kept her eyes shut. Wanted to memorize every detail, every minute of what had just happened, it had been so perfect.

Too restless to sleep after that mind-bending experience taking his wife's innocence, Nate left Mina sleeping and ordered them a light meal in case she woke up hungry. Then he took his laptop back out to the terrace to work.

Resting his head against the back of the sofa, he watched the play of the light on the water. It flickered like flames lapping the blue-black canvas that surrounded him. If he'd anticipated bedding Mina would be more about him ensuring her first time was good for her, he had clearly underestimated his wife's effect on him. How every inch of her inflamed his senses. How every innocent, passionate response to his lovemaking had pulled him deeper and deeper into the web she'd so effortlessly spun around him. Into the incandescent spirit that was Mina.

To go through what she had and emerge with such strength, such belief in the world around her, was remarkable to him. The survivor in her was just as sexy to him as the delectable packaging.

The distant roar of a jet taking off brought his head up. Pierced the almost eerie stillness around him, forcing his brain to admit the truth along with it. He couldn't call what they'd just done sex. Even a man hell-bent on deluding himself would be a fool to make that claim.

He felt something for Mina, something he'd never felt for a woman before. It went beyond the protectiveness he'd initially felt for her to a place deep inside his chest. A place he'd long ago marked forbidden for him.

He knew what it was like to allow yourself to feel, to want things you couldn't have. Because contrary to what his grandfather thought, what Mina had accused him of, he had made an effort to connect with his brother Alex. He had sought him out, made tentative overtures when he'd begun his tenure at Di Sione Shipping, thinking they had been similar animals— wounded beasts who had made themselves into warriors. Perhaps to attempt to put his and his brother's dark past to rest. Only to have Alex shut him down cold. As if he wasn't good enough to breathe the same air as him.

His fingers tightened around the steel casing of his laptop—the tool he used to command an empire built brick by brick by his need to prove none of it mattered to him. That he could shine the brightest.

Some days he managed to convince himself it was true. On others, his past ate away at his insides, slowly but surely corroding his soul. The price he paid for choosing the life he had.

The smoky trail of the departing jet dissolved into the sky, a wisp of gray against black. Mina's dark, dark eyes as he'd taken her filled his head. The *wonder* in them at what they created together. He was playing a dangerous game with her. He knew it. As inevitable as it seemed, the rules he'd insisted on seemed more important than ever.

He had nothing to offer Mina except what his tutelage and position could provide in the way of a successful transition into a business career when their year was up. Some other man would give Mina the happily-ever-after she craved, the *unconditional love*.

Confining himself to the mutual satisfaction they'd promised each other was the only way forward. Or he would break her heart. Not an option when his wife's heart had already been shattered one too many times.

CHAPTER TEN

Everything felt different after Mina's earth-shattering night with Nate. The world seemed to come into a bright, intense focus as they toured the island with the resort manager and viewed the enhancements that had been recently made, all of it so much more vividly real to her than it had been before. As if Nate had awoken part of her sensory being she'd never tapped into before. Hadn't even known existed.

The extent to which she *hadn't* been living was thrown into stark relief. Anger at herself for allowing it to happen, for allowing her mother to rule her life, became a thankfulness that she had finally taken control of her destiny. It made her determined to seize every moment and relish it.

Another disconcerting reality came to light during those heady two days in the Maldives. She was falling for Nate. *Hard.* Something she'd said she wouldn't do. She tried to tell herself it *must* be part of the knight in shining armor fantasy she'd built around him. For what he'd given her—the precious freedom to pursue her life on her own initiative. But she worried it was much, much more than that.

And how unwise was that? she thought as they flew across the world to New York—her new home. To allow herself to fall for a man who had no interest in a permanent relationship with anyone. Who would run in the opposite direction if he knew her feelings.

She stole a glance at her husband as he frowned over a report in the seat beside her. She wasn't even sure how it had happened. Perhaps it had been when he'd claimed her innocence with such achingly tender care. When she'd seen in his dark eyes an equally emotional response to what she'd been feeling. As if what they shared was as rare and monumental as it seemed.

And perhaps that was just in her imagination.

She gave her head a shake and picked up her steaming mug of what you could barely call coffee. To try and convince herself Nate had feelings for her would be making an even bigger mistake than she'd already made. Better to bury whatever infatuation she'd developed deep and use her mental energy to fortify herself for her introduction to New York.

Already the tabloids had caught wind of her and Nate's nuptials. It seemed one of the employees at the Grand Hong Kong had given a reporter a scoop on the real-estate magnate's new marital status. The reporter had dug a bit into Mina's aborted vows in Palermo and had dubbed her *"Nate's stunning runaway Sicilian bride."*

Her stomach rolled. She had the social skills to assume the role of Nate's high-society wife, but she had a feeling her level of sophistication would prove woefully inadequate when it came to the circles he traveled in. And then there was the coming challenge of proving herself in her new marketing role...

She gave an inward shiver. She'd never been to America. Had never visited the intimidating city of New York she knew only from movies. It seemed full of slickly dressed businesspeople who talked fast and had extremely dry senses of humor.

What would they make of her?

"Stop fretting," Nate murmured. "Or I will be forced to find a way to divert you."

The glitter in his heavy-lidded gaze brought every cell in her body to instant attention. "I'm not fretting." His brow lifted. "*Ebbene*, I am," she conceded. "What if my coworkers don't like me? What if your friends, the press, don't like me?"

His gaze softened. "They will love you because you have an innate charm that will win everyone over, Mina. And you are talented. Be yourself and you'll be fine."

She held that close to her heart as they landed at a small private airfield in New Jersey and climbed into the car that was waiting for them. Nate made a phone call to his grandfather to see if they could drop by and show him the ring before the workweek started. When he ended the call, his face was dark.

"He hasn't been well this week."

Her heart squeezed. "Should we go another time?"

"A short visit is fine. He's anxious to see the ring."

Traffic was thick on the highway, slowing to almost a crawl. Mina took the ring out of her purse and studied the beautiful, priceless sapphire.

"You said the Fountain Ring was once Giovanni's? Why did he have to sell it?"

"He came to America from Italy following the Second World War with only the clothes on his back. He needed to sell it to make his start here."

She turned the ring over. "It has an inscription on the inside. I saw it in Pasquale's office. *'Mistress of my heart—BA.'*"

He frowned and took it from her. "Those aren't Giovanni's initials."

She thought about it. "Perhaps they aren't initials. Perhaps it's some sort of a message to a lover?"

Nate thought about that as they made the rest of the slow trip to Long Island. *Had Giovanni had a lover he'd left behind in Italy?* It fit to some extent with the items his siblings had recovered, all of them precious mementos you might give to a lover.

Or perhaps they had nothing to do with an old love affair and were all distinct, separate memories his grandfather had for different times and places of his life?

Giovanni had been married to his wife, Maria, for almost twenty-five years, happy enough from what he'd discerned. But his grandfather was a mystery. Had always been. He had a feeling there was a lot more to know about the legendary shipping tycoon than what he'd revealed.

The clue to his grandfather's past rattled around his brain until they arrived at the Di Sione villa. The doctor was just leaving.

"Keep it brief," he said. "He needs the rest."

A tightness seized Nate's chest. "Is there a revised timeline?"

The doctor shook his head. "He has good weeks and bad. This one was tough. The drugs are helping with the pain but they're also sedating him."

Nate led Mina up the ornate, finely carved staircase to Giovanni's suite of rooms. He held up a hand for her to wait at the door, then ventured inside. His grandfather was lying in the massive mahogany bed, looking heart-droppingly small. Propped up by a mound of pillows, his eyes were half-closed. "Nathaniel," he said, his voice low and raspy. "Did you bring your new wife?"

The tabloids. Nate nodded and beckoned to Mina. "I'd like you to meet my grandfather Giovanni. Giovanni, it was Mina's family who owned the ring."

Giovanni sat up straighter. Gestured for Mina to come closer, then pressed a kiss against her cheek. "I thought I must be hallucinating when I read the newspaper story. Although I knew Nate would fall hard when he met the right one."

Mina smiled. "It all happened rather quickly."

"Did you really leave your fiancé at the altar?"

"*Sì.* Nate and I...it was love at first sight."

"As it should be," said Giovanni, a distant look in his eyes. "It's the way of great love."

Mina's smile faltered. His grandfather didn't notice, his eyes trained on the box she held. "May I see the ring?"

She handed it to him. Giovanni removed the spectacular sapphire from the box. "Exactly as I remembered," he murmured, setting it on his palm and staring at it. "Funny how something precious can be lost to you through the passage of time, but a stone like this? It will be with us always."

Nate wanted desperately to ask his grandfather what the ring meant to him. But Giovanni had already made it clear he wasn't willing to share that information.

"Can I keep it for a few days?" his grandfather asked.

Mina nodded. "I cannot sell it to you until a year is up, as I'm sure Nate has told you. It was a condition my father made when he bequeathed it to me."

His grandfather nodded, shut the box and blinked rapidly. Nate stared hard at him as a tear rolled down Giovanni's weathered face. A fist reached in and clenched his heart. He had never seen Giovanni cry. Not once.

"I am very tired," said his grandfather. "I hope you will forgive me if I keep our visit short today?"

Nate nodded, his throat tight. "Of course."

His grandfather clasped his hand around his wrist and drew him close. "She's lovely. Be happy, Nate."

He opened his mouth to tell him he would visit again during the week, but the emotion clogging his throat made it impossible.

He rested his forehead against his grandfather's. "I love you," he whispered.

Giovanni's fingers tightened around his. Something

ripped loose in Nate's chest, casting him adrift in a stormy sea that threatened to swallow him whole. He turned and walked out of the room before it did.

Nate delivered Mina to his penthouse on the fifty-fifth floor of the Grand New York, a marquee space with sweeping vistas of the city. "Let Rosa know if you need anything," he said, showing her the suite he'd allocated for her.

They were the first words he'd issued since he'd walked out of his grandfather's house, his emotions too big for his heart to hold.

Leaving her to unpack, he went into his study and stood staring out the window at a gray Manhattan. The rage that rose inside of him was so swift and all-encompassing it blurred his vision. Blinded him to anything but the need to strike back. To escape the pain tearing his insides apart.

A sweep of his hand across his desk sent papers flying: contracts, letters of intent, reports on how much money he was worth. When that wasn't satisfying enough he picked up his CEO of the Year award and hurled it at the wall. A hand-carved glass paperweight followed it.

Chest heaving, he rested his palms on his desk, hung his head and cursed himself for taking everything for granted. For assuming this charmed life of his, which was in fact a hollow, poor excuse for an existence, could make up for wanting things that had never been his. For keeping his grandfather at a distance when

Giovanni had offered him everything his pride would not allow him to take.

The love his father had refused to give him. The chance to *belong* to something bigger than the lonely existence he had led.

Except even the all-powerful Giovanni could not wipe away the wounds a tragedy had left behind. The dysfunction his father and Anna's volatile relationship had wreaked. He and his Di Sione siblings were proof of that.

"Nate."

He levered himself away from the desk to find Mina standing in the doorway, eyes wide, hands clenched at her sides.

"Leave me alone."

"Nate—"

"Leave me the hell alone."

Her face paled. She turned on her heel and left.

Mina finished unpacking in the suite Nate had appointed her, eyes burning, heart thumping. The verbal slap he'd administered stung. He was hurting. Hadn't said two words since they'd left Long Island. Then that *display* just now…the loss of his supreme control. The animallike pain in his eyes.

She wanted to help him, to comfort him. But Nate was a solitary animal. He didn't want her in his head. He didn't want her sharing his pain. He wanted to bury it until he went off like a time bomb.

The last of her suits hung up, she scooped her lacy underwear into a drawer. He'd made that part of their arrangement clear. *Don't expect intimacy from me.* It was just sex.

But she couldn't deny it hurt. Couldn't deny it stung after three nights of sleeping in his arms. Of sensing an emotional connection between them that was, perhaps, only in her own head.

Leaning against the exquisite hand-carved cherrywood dresser, she raked a hand through her hair. Breathed past the painful squeeze of her chest. *What was she doing?* Allowing herself to get pulled in even deeper with feelings for a man she couldn't have. Shouldn't want to have.

An affair was all it was supposed to have been. To experience everything she'd missed with a worldly, exciting man who made her toes curl. Allowing herself to develop feelings for Nate when he would walk away from her when his attention span waned was setting herself up for a fall. To have something she so desperately wanted and to once again be left alone was too much of a threat to the fragile sense of worth she'd acquired.

It would prove she was not lovable enough to keep. *Not good enough.* And she was never going there again. Ever.

Pushing away from the dresser, she walked past Nate's study. It was empty, the penthouse silent. He must have gone out, his usual pattern of walking when his emotions grew too great to bear.

Finding her way back to the gleaming stainless steel showpiece of a kitchen, she poured herself a glass of water and took it out to the terrace. The vast concrete and steel metropolis that spread out in front of her was gray and forbidding. A hazy layer of smog sat over the buildings like an embrace; the air felt gritty, harsh in her lungs; and beeping horns, whistles and sirens blended together in a chaotic symphony that would surely keep her up all night.

A wave of longing descended over her. For the vibrant blue sea and sky. The taste of salt air on her lips...

"Not a very good introduction." Strong hands slid around her waist and drew her back against Nate's hard body. "But it can be very beautiful and alive. Give it a day and it will pass."

Her spine remained rigid. He drew her closer, his lips nuzzling her nape. "I shouldn't have taken my anger out on you. I'm sorry."

She softened. "You were hurting."

"Yes. I thought I had dealt with my emotions, but clearly I hadn't."

"You love him. This isn't going to be easy for you."

Silence stretched. "I hadn't told him I loved him until today. It hit me that I could have lost him and he would never have known."

She twisted around in his arms. "He knows. You only have to see you two together to know that."

His mouth flattened, pain darkening his eyes. "I've wasted so much time."

"Then make the most of what you have left. Forge a deeper connection with your siblings."

"We've been through this," he said abruptly. "There is too much baggage there. Too much history to make that happen."

"Says who? Who doesn't want a relationship? You or them?"

His body stiffened. She thought she might have pushed it too far, her muscles tensing for an explosion. A long, silent moment passed. Then he expelled a breath and raked a hand through his hair.

"My mother was my father's secretary. She had an affair with him during a rough patch in his marriage, thinking he loved her, that he would leave his family for her. But that was the way of my father and his wife Anna's relationship. They were big partyers, volatile personalities. They repaired their marriage and my father ended things with my mother. She is a very proud woman. She left her job with Benito and found another. Then she discovered she was pregnant. She couldn't keep the job she'd taken—it was too demanding. She found another but it didn't pay much. My father had made it clear he wanted nothing to do with her. She waited until we were nearly broke before she went to his house one night with me to ask for financial assistance. He shut the door in our faces."

Her breath caught in her throat.

"My father and Anna argued after my mother and I left. They were supposed to attend a party that night, one of those drug-infused affairs of the day where the wealthy blew all their money playing far too hard. My father was notorious for his love of illicit drugs and drink. After their argument, he wrapped their car around a tree and killed himself and Anna."

Oh, mio Dio. "What happened to your siblings?"

"Giovanni took them in."

"But he didn't find out about you until later," she said, remembering. "When Alex found you. How did *he* know about you?"

"He was watching from the window that night. He put two and two together."

She tilted her head to one side and asked the question that had been on her mind since Hong Kong. "Why didn't you bond with your siblings then? That must have been an incredibly emotional experience giving your grandfather his life back."

"Because I didn't want a relationship with them," he said roughly. "I wanted nothing to do with the Di Siones. I couldn't refuse Giovanni's offer to put me through school, to give me a start in business, but that didn't mean I wanted anything to do with a family who'd never acknowledged my existence. Who didn't think I was good enough to be a part of it."

"That wasn't your siblings' fault. It was your father's."

"I made overtures. Overtures which were rebuffed. I knew where I stood."

"Perhaps your siblings have gained a different perspective now." She bit her lip, then plunged into the deep end. "You will regret it if you don't make another attempt. Do you know how much I wish I had brothers and sisters? Yes, maybe they would have come with baggage, but at least they would have been there for me. I would have had *somebody* to lean on."

"This is different." His eyes flashed a warning. "There is no point rehashing a past that can't be changed. Leave it alone, Mina."

She shook her head. "You can't run from your emotions, Nate. Throw away something so valuable. Or what happened today will happen again. Only worse. And then maybe it *will* be too late."

"Mina," he growled, snaking an arm around her waist and dragging her to him. "I said *no more*."

Fury pulsed in his gaze like a living, breathing entity. The hands that held her were full of leashed aggression. Intensity surrounded him like a black cloud. He was seconds away from another explosion.

"Bene," she breathed. *"Bene."*

Her heart tattooed itself against her chest as he slid an arm underneath her knees and picked her up.

"What are you doing?"

"Shutting you up."

Nate carried his wife into his bedroom, a maelstrom of emotion coursing through him. Big emotions, intense emotions Mina managed to pull out of him with that caring, empathetic side of her that never judged, only validated, making him want things he'd long ago decided were impossible.

It was like walking in a minefield, allowing his feelings to surface. To acknowledge just how much his grandfather meant to him. Just how angry he was at himself. Too viciously painful to venture any further into, so he retreated by turning his intensity on the woman he couldn't seem to get enough of. The woman who blanked his brain of anything but her when he came within a five-foot radius of her.

He set Mina down on the floor. "Take off your clothes."

She gave him one of those wide-eyed looks as he

started to strip. He thought she might refuse given the mood he was in. Then heat took hold in her beautiful eyes, the attraction she couldn't fight. The trust she reserved for him no matter what he asked of her.

Her hands moved to the top button of her blouse. She undid the buttons slowly, clumsily, until the last was undone. He watched her the whole time, holding her gaze with his. She unzipped her skirt, pushing it off her hips with a wriggle that turned him hard as stone. Clad in her lacy underwear, her eyes drank him in. Fell to the last piece of clothing he wore. His boxers did nothing to disguise his arousal.

"Come here."

She blinked. Hesitated. Then walked toward him, stopping a couple of inches away. She was so beautiful standing there, so perfectly formed, so highly desirable, his throat went dry.

He nodded his head toward his boxers. "Take them off."

She swallowed convulsively. A silence followed, then she stepped forward, slid her fingers beneath the elastic of his underwear and pushed them down so his pulsing arousal sprang free.

He stepped out of them and kicked them to the side. Gave in to the fantasy that had been raging in his head ever since she'd offered it to him that night in the Maldives. "I have an edge that needs to be taken off," he drawled in a gravelly voice full of need. "If you are so inclined."

A flush spread across her cheeks. His heart pounded painfully in his chest. When she sank to her knees, her dark eyes liquid with desire, the blood roared in his head. *"Sì,"* she murmured. "I am. But you need to tell me if I'm doing it all wrong."

He would have told her that every time she touched him was *right* if his brain had been working. But it had ceased functioning when she'd dropped to her knees.

She took him in her hands and closed her fingers around his shaft. Her tentative, exploratory movements as she worked her way up and down the length of him fired his blood like no practiced touch had ever done. The pleasure that wrote itself across her face as he thickened, lengthened, for her inflamed him. And that was before she took him into the heat of her mouth and just about destroyed him.

He buried his hands in her hair and told her how good it felt. How he wanted it. Where he wanted it. Mina indulged him, seemingly as intoxicated as he was. And then he was there, too fast.

He manacled his fingers around her wrist. "You take more of an edge off," he muttered roughly, in response to the dismayed look on her face, "and it'll be all over."

He bent, picked her up and carried her to the bed. She watched as he rolled on a condom, so much bolder than she'd been that first night. Everything was on display in that face of hers, her open lust for him almost pushing him over the edge.

The mattress depressed as he joined her on the bed. Sinking his palms into her waist he lifted her atop him, his aroused body brushing against her in the most potent of caresses. Mina closed her eyes, allowing him to control the contact. "Nate," she breathed.

Her slick arousal admitted him easily. He brought her down on him, slowly, so she felt every bit of him fill her. Her low moan sent his blood pressure skyrocketing. He wanted, needed, her too much. Needed her to anesthetize his brain as he knew she could.

He flexed his hips and filled her completely. Her gasp split the air. "Okay?" he gritted.

"*Sì.*" Her eyes were glued to his, glazed with pleasure. "It's so *good* like this."

A muttered oath escaped him. He lifted her up and brought her down on him again. Again and again, driving deeper into her slick, tight body with every thrust.

"Nate," Mina cried, her body tightening around his, "*Dio mio*, Nate…"

He wrapped his fingers around her nape and brought her forward until he could see the pleasure exploding in her eyes. "That's it, beautiful," he murmured. "Come for me."

Her eyes went a molten espresso as she contracted around him. The sensation sent him into a mind-blowing climax that made the room rock.

It was long moments before his brain returned to earth, his hands sliding over Mina's ample curves. She arched like a kitten into his touch, her eyes heavy-lidded. "Do you want me to go to my own room?"

His heart lurched at the question. He should take her there. Establish some boundaries from the start so they both had their space. But he'd gotten used to having her in his arms. And since when had resisting Mina gotten him anywhere?

"Stay," he murmured, brushing his lips against her temple. "I'm going to turn out the lights and I'll be back."

She curled into his warmth when he returned, already drifting into unconsciousness as he wrapped himself around her. He tuned out the fact he'd never let another female stay the night in this bed along with the premonition this dangerous game he was playing with his wife was on a course for disaster.

The time for turning back had long passed.

CHAPTER ELEVEN

IF MINA HAD THOUGHT her first few weeks working for Nate had been tough, her first couple at the Brunswick Developments head office were an exercise in survival. Nate's marketing director came exactly as advertised. A tough, native New Yorker, she had little time to pander to the CEO's wife. Not that Mina wanted her to—she wanted exactly the opposite, to stand on her own two feet.

And stand on her own two feet she did, as Carole put her to work immediately with a get-busy-ask-questions-as-you-need-to approach.

After floundering through one project, afraid to appeal to her intimidating new boss for help, Mina started asking questions. She tapped her boss when she needed to and winged it when she could, learning more in those two weeks than she was sure she would have in a year at school.

When Carole capped off her second week with praise for her first complete marketing plan, she thought she'd died and gone to heaven. It was almost enough to banish her nerves as she and Nate drove uptown to his mother's penthouse for the cocktail party she was throwing in their honor.

Nate had put his mother off as long as he could manage to give Mina time to adjust to the city and her new job, but he could stall no longer, so tonight was the night she was to be introduced to the toast of New York society.

The nerve-racking drive with Nate weaving in and out of traffic, combined with her nerves, started to make her feel nauseous. Odd when she didn't ever remember getting carsick, but this was Manhattan they were talking about.

Nate studied her face as they rode the elevator to his mother's apartment. "You okay? You look a little green."

She forced a smile. "Nerves, combined with your driving, I expect."

He put a hand to the wall beside her. "You don't get carsick."

"Not usually."

"Don't be nervous." He cupped the back of her head. "You're stunningly beautiful, Mrs. Brunswick. You'll charm them all."

She wanted to tell him to stop calling her that. That every time he did, every time he kissed her, she fell harder for him. But his lips were on hers then, driving everything from her head. Even the fear she was in love with him.

He lifted his head as the elevator pinged their arrival, his breath mingling with hers. "Now you look the part," he murmured, jabbing a button to keep the doors closed. "Fix your lipstick."

Her makeup repaired, they joined the party. Emily Brunswick, a dynamic, attractive woman in her late fifties Mina had liked from the moment she'd met her, made it her mission to introduce Mina to everyone in the room. Her nausea abated, Mina actually enjoyed herself with Emily easing the way.

She was in the middle of a conversation with her mother-in-law and the director of an art gallery when the strong smell of an hors d'oeuvre turned her stomach. Her nausea resurfaced with a vengeance, a wave of perspiration blanketing her. She had barely enough time to excuse herself and make it to the powder room before her stomach announced its intentions to vacate itself.

When she'd decided the heaving had stopped for good, she got to her feet, splashed water on her face and attempted to repair her makeup.

"Mina?" Nate's voice pierced the wooden door.

She opened it to find him standing there, a frown on his face. "You were sick?"

"No," she denied, "I'm fine."

"You're a terrible liar," he said flatly. "We're leaving."

"But your mother went to all this trouble…"

It was no use. He was already pulling her toward Emily to say good-night. Mina assured Nate's mother she was fine, likely just exhausted, and apologized for cutting the evening short. In the car, she sat through a lecture from Nate about how she shouldn't let things like this get to her.

"I don't think it was the party." She pressed her

head back against the seat. "I was fine after the first few minutes. Your mother is lovely."

He glanced over at her. "A bug, maybe?"

"Probably."

Except she never got stomach sick from bugs. Maybe once in her life. And she never got carsick. The more she thought about it, the colder she got, mixing with the perspiration to make her feel distinctly clammy. *There was no way she could be...*

Her heart seized. She'd gone to a doctor to get birth control pills as soon as she'd arrived in New York to be doubly sure there was no chance she could get pregnant. Because getting pregnant would be a disaster.

Maledizione. She wiped a palm over her brow. She was making herself ill just thinking about it.

Nate put her to bed when they got home and went off to do some email, promising he'd check on her in a few minutes. She rested her head against the pillows and stared blankly out at the spectacular view of New York. She could not be pregnant. It was impossible. Nate wore condoms; she was on the pill, *newly* on the pill but...

She got out of bed. Pulled on yoga pants, a T-shirt and running shoes, grabbed her purse and took the long way around the penthouse to the door to avoid Nate's study. Riding the elevator to ground level, she headed toward the drugstore in the lobby. Surprisingly, enough people must wonder if they're pregnant while on vacation or business trips because the shelves were liberally stocked. Heart pounding, she snatched up two and got into line to pay.

The lineup was five people deep. She tapped her foot impatiently as she waited. Finally, she got to the front of the line, paid and hightailed it back up to the penthouse. Pressing her thumb on the biometric scan, she walked into a solid wall of... *Nate.*

Lurching backward, she shoved the bag behind her. "*Dannazione.* You scared me."

Nate eyed her darkly. "What were you doing roaming the streets while you're sick? Roaming the streets at night, *period*?"

She pulled in a breath. "I needed a...a book. And I wasn't roaming the streets. I went to the store in the building."

"Really?" He nodded toward the hand she had behind her back. "What kind of books are you buying?"

"Not ones you need to see." She went to walk past him. Nate caught her wrist in a firm grip.

"What's in the bag, Mina?"

She cocked her head to one side. "Honestly, can a girl not have a little privacy?"

"Not tonight she can't. Not when you were upending the contents of your stomach into the toilet an hour ago and that's a drugstore bag behind your back."

Her brain worked furiously. "It's an old-fashioned remedy we Sicilians use."

"Fascinating. Show it to me."

"Nate—"

He reached around her with catlike swiftness and plucked the bag out of her hand. Mina pressed her palms to her eyes.

The longest silence of her life followed. She dropped

her hands. Nate was *gray.* "It's just a precaution," she said, talking fast. "It can't possibly be that. My imagination was running away with me and—"

"I used a condom every time. You're on the pill."

"Sì," she said, nodding quickly. "Like I said, it's just a precaution. I only did it because I didn't feel well yesterday, either, and I thought why... Nate," she said, frowning as he turned even grayer, "maybe you should sit down."

He ran his palm over the stubble on his chin. "I think you," he said slowly, handing her the bag, "should go do the tests. One—two—whatever works."

She closed her fingers around the bag. Decided there was nothing else *to* do. She walked with a pounding heart toward the powder room, closed the door and leaned against it. *You can do this.*

Two positive tests later, she was sitting on the decorative love seat in the powder room composing herself when Nate flung the door open. "Out."

She handed the tests to him, walked past him and collapsed on the sofa in the salon. The door to the garbage can thumped shut, a long silence followed and then Nate walked into the salon, headed straight to the bar and poured himself a drink. *Not fair.*

"Mi dispiace," she said quietly.

He gave her a grim look. "Why are you apologizing? It takes two to make a baby."

"Because this is a disaster."

He didn't refute the statement. Instead, he sat down beside her and downed a healthy gulp of the amber liquid in the glass.

"I would never—"

"Stop," he said harshly. "I would never suggest that."

The funny expression on his face caught her off guard. Then she realized what she'd said. Nate had been the result of an unexpected pregnancy...

"I didn't mean—"

"I know you didn't."

The seconds rolled by, the ticking of the clock on the wall excruciatingly loud to Mina's sensitized nerve endings. With every second that passed, with every moment that frozen, dismayed look continued to sit on Nate's face, her heart slipped deeper into despair. He didn't want a relationship, let alone a baby. He was horrified.

She had just attained her freedom, had begun a job she loved. It couldn't be worse timing.

Her head throbbed, blood hammered against her temples. She wanted to feel joy, because surely a baby was a wonderful thing. Instead, she dropped her head in her hands and prayed for this to be a dream she'd wake up from soon.

"Stop panicking," Nate rasped. "We will figure this out."

"How?" She lifted her head. "You can't even be in a relationship, Nate. How are you going to handle being a father?"

"Day by day, step by step. And I think we are already doing a pretty good approximation of a relationship."

"Because you know you can walk away the minute

you feel claustrophobic. The minute your attachment antenna picks up too strong a signal, we're done."

He rested his dark, fathomless gaze on her. "If that were true I would have already cut things off."

So he knew. Knew that she was in love with him. Hot color climbed into her face. "Why haven't you? Why break your rules for me, Nate? Because of that knight in shining armor complex you have for me you deny but is so patently obvious? Because you think I'm so vulnerable I'll break if you do?"

His gaze dropped away from hers. "I don't know."

"Well, I do." Humiliation and pain brought everything spilling out. "You have feelings for me. You won't allow yourself to explore them because you're afraid they'll bring this house of cards you have built tumbling down."

Heat blazed in his eyes. "I have let you in, Mina. I have shared things I've never shared with anyone before."

"Because there's no risk! I'm out the door in a year. You have a built-in out." She waved her arms around her. "None of this is threatening because we're just playing our roles. You're the honorable knight, I'm the damsel in distress. It justifies everything."

He slapped the glass down on the table and glared at her. "What do you want from me? I care about you. You know that. I have opened up my life to you, tried to give you everything you need."

"And I will never be able to repay you for that." She met the frustration burning in his eyes with a lifted chin. "What you have given to me, Nate, is a gift. You walked into my life and not only saved me from Silvio, you saved me from *myself*. From sacrificing my life out of some misguided sense of loyalty to my mother. You have *empowered* me to be the person I knew I could be but was too afraid to realize. But this," she said, pointing at her stomach, "is real. It's our wake-up call. We can't play this game anymore."

He stared at her silently. She sucked in a deep breath, forcing herself to do what he wouldn't. "If you don't see our relationship ever moving past the status quo—that's fine. Honestly, Nate, it's fine. I told you in the beginning I could handle this and I can. I—" she broke off, raking a hand through her hair "—I just need to know."

Ice crackled as he picked up his glass, put it to his mouth and took another long sip. His face was impassive. "We have a good thing, Mina. The way I see it, we don't have much choice in the matter. We make this marriage permanent and do what's right by this child."

Her chest tightened. *Not because he loved her. Not because he wanted her in his life.* "Because you won't see this child abandoned by its father like you were?"

"Because it's the right thing to do." The edge to his voice sliced across her skin in sharp rebuke. "This child deserves the presence of both its parents in its life."

She closed her eyes against the pain in her temples. She'd been afraid to admit she loved him because of this. Because she'd feared her feelings wouldn't be returned. And now she had her answer.

A vision of the soul-destroying kind of a relationship she and Nate would share filled her head. How she would always be secretly hoping he'd learn to love her just as she had done her entire life with her mother, only to have it never be returned.

She wrapped her arms around herself, bile rising in her throat. She couldn't go back to being that lonely, desperate for affection version of herself she'd hated. Not ever again.

"Mina." Nate curled his fingers around her arm. "We are good together. You're flourishing at Brunswick Developments. It makes sense."

She opened her eyes, the affection she saw in his dark gaze driving her misery even deeper. "A loveless marriage isn't an option for me. No matter how practical."

An emotion she couldn't read flickered in his eyes. "This isn't one of those Hollywood movies you love. Being good together can go a long way."

She shook her head. "It wouldn't work. You'd come to resent me. Me and the baby. You said it yourself, a white picket fence existence isn't for you. You're a solitary creature, Nate. You need your space. My feelings for you would sit between us like this awkward thing we both won't address until you'd wished you'd ended it now."

The ensuing silence broke the rest of her heart. "You're not well," he said finally. "Not thinking rationally. We'll talk about this tomorrow."

It wouldn't change anything, she speculated miserably as he put her to bed and left her to no doubt ruminate about what a big mess they'd created. It had been her fault letting herself fall in love with him. Convincing herself he could change when he never would.

CHAPTER TWELVE

MINA WOULD COME AROUND.

It wasn't the first time Nate had told himself that on a dull, gray Manhattan afternoon, days after his and Mina's fruitless discussion about their future had ended in stalemate.

It had taken him that long to emerge from the numbness that had invaded his brain, the complete sense of unreality that had taken over his life. *He was going to be a father.* The one challenge he'd been sure he'd never take on. Had never wanted to take on.

Restless as he waited for a call from the West Coast that was now five minutes behind schedule, he pushed his chair back from his desk, got up and walked to the elegantly cased, floor-to-ceiling windows designed to provide maximum light to his sleek, darkly furnished office space. Gray New York in the dog days of winter didn't help his mood.

Further contemplation hadn't crystallized his and Mina's situation. The only thing he'd been able to coherently articulate to his wife in the strained conversations they'd had was his sense of responsibility when it came to their child. He would never allow his son or daughter to grow up without a father. He would stand by Mina and this child, he would give up the freedom he cherished so greatly and he would do his best by both of them.

That had to be enough.

As for the gray areas? His feelings for Mina. Her demand he address them. His confusion on all of the above. Avoidance had been his strategy. When Mina saw reason, that they were good together, that they were better off raising this child together, it would all sort itself out. Pushing himself into saying things he'd regret, making promises he couldn't keep, was not how he was going to play this.

Walking to his desk, he buzzed through to Josephine. "Can you find out why the West Coast call is late?"

"Will do. Oh, Nate?"

"Mmm?"

"Mina left early. Said she'd see you at home."

He frowned. "Was she not feeling well?"

"She seemed fine. A little pale, maybe. She's been working long hours."

He sat down at his desk after Jo went to chase his call. Mina always waited for him. She always had more than enough work to do. Was she not feeling well?

This morning she'd been unusually silent in the car as they'd driven in. She'd been off, in her own head since the revelation she was pregnant, but this morning had been different. She'd been completely distant.

An uneasy feeling working its way through him,

he got to his feet, collected his jacket, grabbed his briefcase and stopped by Jo's desk. "I'll take the call in the car."

His sense that something was wrong grew as he sat in gridlocked traffic. By the time he walked into the penthouse he was cranky and worried. Stalking through the salon he found his wife in her bedroom. Absorbed the neatly packed suitcase on the floor.

"What is *that*?"

Mina folded the sweater she'd been holding and dropped it into the case. Her hands clenched by her sides as she absorbed his aggressive stance. "I'm leaving."

He stepped closer, a buzzing sound filling his head. "*Where* exactly are you going?"

"Paris. I'm going to stay with Celia for a bit."

A seething anger, a fury he couldn't explain, spread through him. "Is this what you do? Run from everything?"

Her eyes darkened. "*That* is not fair."

He jammed his hands on his hips. "We can make this work, Mina. If you'd stop living in that fairy-tale world of yours and accept the fact that love is this mythological concept you women create that lasts exactly as long as the pheromones do."

She lifted her chin. "My *mamma* told me the night before my wedding, the night Silvio hit me, that life is not all sunshine and rainbows. Well, I disagree. I want that. I'd rather have a few years of wonderful than never knowing love at all."

Dear God. He expelled a breath. "So you're just

going to give up the opportunity of a lifetime at Brunswick Developments, jet off to Paris and then what?"

"I was hoping you would help me with a job at the Grand in Paris."

A heavy feeling weighted his stomach. *She was serious.*

"I live here. When am I going to see my child?"

She gave him an even look. "You live on your jet. Even if I was in New York you'd rarely be home. You can come to Paris just as easily."

He pushed a hand through his hair. He didn't like the idea of her being an ocean away, and it didn't all have to do with the baby. "You don't have to work, regardless of what we do."

"I want to." Her gaze held his. "All of this, *everything* you've given me, has shown me how much I want this. To stand on my own two feet. To go after my dreams and make my father proud. It won't be easy with this baby, but I'll make it work."

Reluctant admiration cooled his ire. "Why don't you just stay?" he said softly. "Don't throw away the life you've started to build. We'll find you your own place."

"Because you're here." Her mouth quivered with the admission. "Because I love you. You know I do. It would kill me to see you with other women because I know how it feels to have something so perfect now. To know I can have that with you. And I can't settle for anything less."

His heart stopped in his chest. He inhaled, tried to pull a breath in. "Mina—"

"Let me go," she said softly. "Let me be the gladiator you taught me to be."

He wished in that moment he had never taught her that damn analogy. That she didn't have the strength to walk away, because he didn't have the guts to stop her. Not when the price was opening himself up to all the pain the world had to offer. To the disillusionment in Mina's eyes when she discovered how empty he really was inside.

"Okay," he said. "I'll have the Grand contact you. When is your flight?"

The shattered look in her eyes almost unmanned him. "It's a red-eye tonight. I was going to take a cab. There's no need for you to drive me."

Tonight? A sharp stab of pain lanced through him. "I'll drive you," he said roughly. "Tell me when you're ready."

Traffic was surprisingly light for a weekday evening. They got to the airport in record time. Nate pulled the car up in front of the busy departures entrance and got out to help a pale Mina with her luggage.

"Are you sure you're fit to travel?"

"I have the medicine the doctor gave me in my purse." Mina reached up to press a kiss against his cheek, looking so small and vulnerable it was all he could do not to haul her against him and forbid her to go. "I'll text you when I get to Celia's."

Don't let her go. A voice inside his head said it would be the biggest mistake he ever made. But the survival instinct in him was stronger. He opened his mouth to say something, *anything*, but she was already turning on her heel and walking away.

She did not look back.

He got into the car and watched her disappear into the terminal. Thought about that day she'd opened up the door to him in Palermo, a vision in white in her beautiful wedding dress. His for the taking. How he wasn't man enough to claim the gift that she was.

Nate finished his second Scotch in the quiet, oppressive confines of the penthouse and considered a third. Splayed out in his favorite chair, his eyes on the New York skyline, he tried to block out the delicate scent of Mina's perfume still lingering in the air. How her presence seemed to be everywhere. In his head. In his heart.

When the valet had asked after her tonight upon his return, he'd just looked at him dumbly as if the young college student had asked him why the moon was yellow.

He was in love with her. Had been for weeks. *He* who didn't even believe in the concept of the word. Or perhaps, more accurately, rejected it for what it had come to symbolize. *Pain, rejection, heartache.*

The emptiness he felt now was different from the constant, recurring version of it that had characterized his life. The knowledge that perhaps he could be whole if he had Mina made it particularly acute. Because he had been happy with her for the first time in his life.

He'd embarked on this three-act play of a marriage with her with the caveat it wasn't real. It was all about the end goal—a ring for his grandfather to make him happy in his dying days, and a new life for Mina. When, in fact, everything about them had been real.

Instead of facing the truth—instead of facing his feelings for Mina head-on—he'd decided to allow the story to run to its inevitable conclusion. Hoping he'd never have to make a conscious decision, an admission about how he felt about his wife.

Except Mina had called his bluff. He might have taught her how to be a warrior, but *she* had taught him survivors like them had to fight their inner battles, too. Disarm the defenses they'd constructed to have a chance at a future that transcended their past. In that, she was way ahead of him.

She had given him precious months with Giovanni, had taught him to acknowledge his feelings would not destroy him—they would free him. And yet he had let her walk away. As if he could exist without her now. *Hell.* He scowled and reached for the bottle.

He had the cap off before he stopped, screwed it back on and picked up the phone.

"Nate." Surprise edged Alex's voice. "What's up?"

"Can we meet for a drink?"

"Now?"

"Now. Tomorrow. Whatever works."

A pause. "Sure. You want to meet at that new place in the Ritz?"

Thirty minutes later, he was sliding into a chair opposite his elder brother in the upscale bar that overlooked Central Park.

"Nate." Alex nodded at him in that measured way of his.

"Alex."

As dark-featured as he was, with the same designer stubble and hard edge, the resemblance between the two of them was unmistakable. But it went deeper than the cosmetics—right down to their personalities, which tended toward the moodier side of the spectrum.

Alex moved his gaze over Nate's rumpled shirt and hair. "You look like you could use a drink."

"Might as well continue my momentum."

His brother flagged a waiter and asked for a bottle of Scotch. A wary silence followed.

"Thank you for coming," Nate said at last. "How did your mission for Giovanni go?"

"I have the painting. And a princess."

"A *princess*?"

"A long story. The painting—the portrait—Giovanni sent me to retrieve is of Lucia, the exiled queen of Isola D'Oro. A very *intimate* painting of her." Alex shook his head. "But why Giovanni wanted it…it makes me wonder, might he have a whole past we know nothing about?"

Nate frowned. "While I was in Sicily I had a PI do a search for the Di Sione family. There is no trace of Giovanni. Not only in Livorno, *nowhere* in Italy."

Alex nodded. "Maybe we'll find out the truth now that Giovanni has all the pieces of the puzzle back. You managed to retrieve yours?"

"Yes, the ring. Mina noticed an inscription on the ring. *'Mistress of my heart—BA.'*"

The waiter arrived with the Scotch. Alex paused, taking this in before he poured them both a hefty portion.

Alex frowned. "Who is BA?"

"I have no idea."

"I have a feeling," Alex said, tipping his glass against Nate's, "you asked me here to talk about more than Giovanni."

Nate took a long swallow of Scotch, set the glass down and lifted his gaze to his brother's. "Mina's pregnant."

Alex's eyes widened. "Congratulations... I *think*."

"I want to know about Benito," Nate said abruptly. "What kind of a father was he? What kind of a man was he?"

"Deeply flawed." His brother sat back in his chair and brought his Scotch with him. "He and Giovanni had issues we were never privy to. My father refused to work with him at Di Sione Shipping. He started business after failed business Giovanni kept funding but nothing ever stuck."

"His partying and drug habits didn't help, I'm sure."

Alex nodded. "My mother cleaned herself up. Exchanged her drug and alcohol habit for a shopping addiction. But we were never a *family*. Neither of them had any interest in being parents. The nannies raised us."

All the pieces started to lock into place in Nate's head. Why all his siblings had struggled so much.

"You're afraid you won't be a good father," Alex speculated, his gaze narrowing on his. "Because you never had one. Because my father was the man he was."

"Isn't that the way it goes?" Nate rasped, lifting his glass to his lips. "Lead by example…"

"Except you have a mother who loves you, something we Di Siones never had. Someone who inspired you to reach for your dreams, who shaped you into the man that you are. Your name is the key to entry to any boardroom on this planet, Nate, and yet I think the big chip you carry around on your shoulder affects your self-perception." He pointed his glass at Nate. "I should know, I carry one myself."

Nate blinked. Absorbed his brother's words. "When I reached out to you when I started at Di Sione, I thought we had a lot in common, you and I. But you blew me off. Acted as if I wasn't fit to breathe the same air as you."

"It was difficult for me," he conceded. "You were a reminder of that night…the night my parents died. Of my own failure. To you. Keeping you a secret might have been easier for me but I'm sure it was hell on you. Seeing you there…watching my grandfather attempting to atone for my sins was difficult."

Nate shook his head. "I was never comfortable with that. I think his vaulting me ahead in the company was Giovanni's way of making up for the past. But I never wanted it."

"I know. But I couldn't handle it then. I was young and anger was a lot easier to feel than guilt. Hell, it still is."

Nate was silent for a long moment. "I'm sorry," he said finally, "that it worked out that way."

Alex shook his head. "It's me who should be apologizing. You reached out to me when you needed an ally and I wasn't there for you. I regret that now. I regret a lot of things."

Nate sat back and absorbed the epiphany that had just transpired. How everything you thought you knew was, in fact, not so clear-cut. That life had layers you had to burrow through to find the truth. How his self-perception was indeed flawed.

"Life is complex," he said. "*Relationships* are complex."

Alex lifted his glass in a toast, a cynical smile curving his lips. "Welcome to the Di Siones. The most dysfunctional clan on the planet."

Something shifted inside of Nate as he touched his glass to his brother's. A hope, perhaps, that the future could be different.

"When do I get to meet Mina?"

"I'm not sure that's going to happen." He set his glass down and flicked his brother a glance. "She's on a plane to Paris as we speak."

"You want to talk about it?"

"You got all night?"

His brother nodded toward the Scotch. "Why do you think I got a bottle?"

CHAPTER THIRTEEN

MINA FIGURED GLADIATORS were allowed to cry if they had a really, really good reason for it.

Walking away from the man you loved while he stood there and watched you do it seemed worthy enough, particularly when the end of your affair had driven home how very deluded you were. How the emotions you'd been so convinced the man in question felt for you had been nothing more than a display of honor on his part, the very same honor he'd been demonstrating from the beginning. And weren't you stupid to have thought it was more than that?

She had done the right thing, she told herself on the long flight from New York to Paris on which she'd miraculously been upgraded, her husband's influence no doubt. She had tried to see the practicality of remaining married to Nate that last week with him, putting her head down at work and burying herself in her assignments. But watching Nate struggle to pretend he was happy about becoming a father and permanent husband when it was so clearly anathema to him had been too painful to stand.

She would get over Nate in time. But if she'd stayed, he would have claimed more and more of her soul every day, until he'd had all of her. Until it would have been impossible for her to leave. Both of them would have begun to hate each other for what they wanted and could never have.

She thought she'd pretty much gotten herself together by the time Celia picked her up at the airport and drove her home to her beautiful, old apartment in the heart of Paris. But after her best friend had demanded a full recap, the tears had started anew.

"Don't waste any more time on him," Celia had stated in that blunt, very French way of hers. "Men are like seasons. They come and they go. I have my book club this week. Read the book, enjoy some good gossip and it will be all better."

Mina read the book, lounged on Celia's sofa and ate copious amounts of cheese and crackers to keep the nausea at bay. By the time the book club was assembled in Celia's tiny salon on Monday, crowded into every remaining space, she was doing a better job at hiding her heartbreak.

Brigitte, the last remaining member of the group, was arriving late from a work event. When the buzzer went off at seven, Celia opened the door, still talking, her words dying on her lips when she saw who it was. The blood drained from Mina's face.

"This is a book club," Celia said to Nate, recovering faster than Mina did. "No men allowed."

Nate blinked. "What book are you reading?"

"The Age of Innocence."

"Can't help you there." He pointed the bouquet of fresh flowers he held at Mina. "I was hoping I could take you for dinner."

Dinner? He had somehow materialized in Paris and wanted her to go to dinner with him? She stared at the man she'd cried too many tears over, dark and dangerous in jeans and a leather jacket.

Swallowing hard, she found her voice. "I'm afraid I'm not in the market for a knight in shining armor."

His gaze speared hers. "How about a man who deeply regrets watching the best thing that's ever happened to him walk out of his life? Who wants to replay this from the beginning, this time for real? No one saving anyone, Mina, no Hollywood reenactments, just the raw, unadulterated truth."

Her breath caught in her throat. The girl beside her set her paperback down. "This is better than the book."

"You don't want him," the beautiful blonde on her other side murmured, "I'll take him."

That brought Mina to her feet. She collected her wrap from the sofa and crossed the room to Nate on legs that felt like spaghetti. He'd missed a button on his shirt, heavy dark stubble covered his jaw and the slightly askew, spiky hairstyle he wore looked a bit… *undone*.

Her heart squeezed. Nate handed the flowers to Celia with his most charming smile. "Would you?"

"Oui," she said curtly, giving him a long look. "You hurt her. I hurt you."

Nate captured Mina's hand in his in the car that sat

waiting for them at the entrance. *Guard your heart*, she told herself. *You haven't heard what he has to say yet.* But the tense, hard line of her husband's jaw kept her palm in his. She had never seen Nate nervous. Ever.

They pulled up in front of the Grand Paris a short time later. A trademark glass elevator sent them swishing to Nate's rooftop penthouse. Nate guided her out onto the terrace where a table was set for two, a sparkling view of Paris as a backdrop.

Mina sank down on one of the sofas in the lounge area, her gaze on her husband's tense face. "What did you mean by us 'replaying this from the beginning'?"

He sat down beside her. "You forgot 'the raw, unadulterated truth.'"

"Nate…"

He expelled a breath. "When I was five I asked my mother why I didn't have a father like all the other kids I knew. She told me mine had another family—that he loved me very much, but he couldn't take care of us both. I accepted that with the innocence of a five-year-old, but I kept asking when he was going to come visit. Eventually I stopped when he never came.

"The night my mother took me to my father's house was the first time I'd met him. I was wary, *excited*, curious—every emotion in the book. I had this picture of him in my head. Then he opened the door, took one look at my mother and me and told us to get off his property."

She laced her fingers through his and squeezed.

"My mother begged him to listen, to help us. He

told her to stop lying. That she was a slut who wanted to take his money with a child that wasn't his."

Her jaw dropped open. "How could he do that?"

"He wasn't in his right mind. Anna came to the door, all hell broke loose. My mother was scared. We left and went home. I remember thinking, was he lying, had my mother lied to me? She put me to bed. I could hear her crying. It hurt so much I willed myself to sleep. I woke up in the middle of the night, my bed covered in vomit."

She tightened her fingers around his, her heart breaking for him.

"I'm not telling you this for your pity. I'm telling you this because I watched my mother, the strongest person I know, die that night. She worked two jobs to put food on the table. She kept our family in one piece, but she was never the same person after that. She still *loved him*."

"And you decided you would never make yourself that vulnerable to a woman."

"To anyone. I quit school, I worked the streets with a gang. I was headed for a bad place when Alex came and found me. I had a choice to choose the right or wrong path then and luckily I had Giovanni to guide me. I channeled my obsession with proving my father wrong about me into my career. I would become so successful *no one* could ignore me. But my first year at Di Sione Shipping wasn't easy. I felt out of my depth. Adrift in a foreign world.

"Alex and I—we seemed cut from the same cloth. Not the worlds we lived in, of course, but we were both struggling with our pasts—wounded beasts trying to make ourselves into warriors. I approached him one night and asked him out for a beer. He looked at me as if I were nothing."

Her heart throbbed. He had been rejected not once, but twice, by the Di Siones.

He shook his head. "It wasn't Alex's fault. Giovanni had put us in an awkward position, vaulting me forward in the company and leaving Alex to climb the ranks. Alex felt guilty for keeping my existence a secret. There were a lot of layers to our relationship."

"But I should not have pushed you when I didn't know the whole story."

"You were *right* to push me. I called Alex. We had a drink. It's far from perfect, but it's a start."

A wet heat stung the backs of her eyes. Nate brushed his thumb across her cheek, his eyes softening. "I have been running away from this thing between us because you made me want what I had told myself was impossible—you, a relationship with my siblings, everything I'd accepted I could never have. You were willing to be a gladiator—to fight for what you wanted—but I was not."

A tear slipped down her face. "You're the one who gave me that."

"No," he said, wiping the tear away with his thumb. "The strength you have comes from inside you. You are a survivor. You have chosen to rise above your past. All I did was show you how to use it. Whereas I," he said, his mouth twisting, "used my past as an excuse to withdraw. I refused to believe in the concept of love because to me loving, making yourself vulnerable, has only meant pain in my life.

"I convinced myself what I felt for you was all about the protective instincts I had," he continued, "because admitting I cared for you, admitting I loved you, meant letting you in. Allowing you to see the broken, empty part of me I have never shown to anyone. The part," he said, his eyes on hers, "I was afraid you would reject."

Her vision blurred, tears running down her cheeks in a steady stream now. "We're all broken, Nate. Every single one of us. It's what we do once we acknowledge it that matters."

He nodded. "I went to talk to Alex because I'm scared to death of being a father. I had no example set for me. Had no idea even what kind of a father my own was. Which didn't help matters, because he was, apparently, no kind of a father. But what I do know," he said, a determined glitter in his eyes, "is that I want to be a father to our baby. To do the best job I can."

She swallowed hard, thinking how badly she'd misinterpreted his fear. "You don't think I'm frightened? That I don't wonder the same thing with a mother like mine?"

He reached for her and gathered her onto his lap. "You will be a great mother *because* of your past, not in spite of it. You've used the challenges in your life to make you stronger, not weaker. And you will give that strength of spirit to our child."

She traced the hard line of his jaw with her fingers. "What about your need for freedom? What if you end up resenting me and the baby and want your life back?"

His gaze darkened. "It won't happen. I haven't slept this week. Haven't eaten. Because you weren't there. I *need* you in my life, Mina."

She ran her finger down the front of his shirt. "I noticed you missed a button. You're looking a little disheveled."

He ignored the tease, lifting her chin with his finger. "So," he said roughly, "you have the unvarnished truth now. Your human connection project is complete. Tell me if you still want me, Mina, because if you say yes now, it's forever."

"Do you have to ask?" she said softly. "Your human side only makes you more attractive, Nate Brunswick. And I was already falling over myself for you the first time I met you."

The tension in his face eased. "You were ridiculously sexy in your maid outfit."

"And you were *very, very* improper."

He brought his mouth down to hers. "You loved every minute of it."

"*Sì.* I did."

He kissed her then, a long, slow kiss that cemented the promises they'd made to each other under a clear, star-strewn Paris sky. That they would rise above their pasts and grasp this chance at happiness with both hands. Two survivors who'd learned that destiny was not a foregone conclusion—it was all in the choices they made.

She hadn't been wrong, Mina thought, wrapping

her arms around her husband's neck and kissing him back. She had been so very, very right.

She was a gladiator, after all. Faith was a prerequisite.

EPILOGUE

New York—nine months later

THE HISTORIC THIRTEENTH-CENTURY Gothic cathedral on Manhattan's west side glimmered with an almost ethereal light as the late-afternoon sun pressed against its elaborate, showstopping stained glass windows.

It was almost enough to match the incandescent glow filling Mina as Nate slid a diamond-studded eternity band on her finger to join the ring he'd placed there a year ago on that tumultuous, emotion-filled day in Palermo which had changed their lives.

This time as she stepped toward him and lifted her face for his kiss, the reconfirming of their vows complete, there were no nerves involved, no questions about her future, only the butterflies in her stomach that came with a kiss from her husband, butterflies she suspected would never go away.

"Enough sunshine and rainbows for you?" Nate murmured against her lips.

"Sì," she returned huskily, curving her fingers around his jaw and lifting up on tiptoe for his kiss.

The priest coughed as the expression of affection went on a fraction too long. Laughter danced in Nate's eyes as he lifted his head. "Have to up my game."

Mina stepped back, the glow inside of her almost too much to contain. The ceremony concluded, she collected two-month-old Giovanni Vincenzo Brunswick from Natalia to make their walk down the aisle.

The Di Sione clan looked on approvingly on their left, a miraculous feat to have them all in one place. Mina's mother, her *nonna*, a handful of her cousins and Celia sat on the right, the intimate, private ceremony to cement their vows what she and Nate had both wanted.

A reception followed at the Brunswicks' Westchester estate, which did not feature a white picket fence, but did include lavish gardens little Giovanni could someday play in, and a koi pond Mina loved. Much wine was consumed and a great deal of laughter filled the fairy-tale gardens as the Di Siones and Mastrantinos mixed, her mother thankfully on her best behavior.

It warmed Mina's heart to watch her husband with his half siblings. He was gradually letting his guard down—forging deeper relationships with all of them, particularly Alex, who did seem so much in character like Nate. The party lasted into the wee hours, until finally, her husband gave the guests some pointed glances, everyone headed for their cars and they went inside to relieve the nanny from her duties.

Giovanni, so very tiny Mina had been terrified to touch him at first, was sound asleep, his fist shoved in his mouth. Nate ran a finger down the baby's cheek, the glitter in his eyes saying everything he found it hard to verbalize. He had fallen instantly in love with their son, would sometimes stand there fascinated, watching him until Mina had to call him to bed.

But not tonight. "I thought they were never going to leave," he growled, switching off the light and propelling her from the room.

"They were having fun."

She toed off her shoes in their room, her heartbeat kicking up at the look of primal hunger on her husband's face. Stepping toward him, she presented him with her back so he could unzip her dress.

His fingers dispensed with the zipper, his mouth consuming a mouthful of her bare shoulder. "Are you exhausted?"

Usually she was. She'd wanted to be a hands-on mother despite the permanent position she'd taken in the Brunswick Developments marketing department, which had meant collapsing into bed at night for the last few weeks since she'd been back to work—weeks in which the doctor had finally cleared her and Nate to be intimate again. Not ideal when Nate's primary strength wasn't patience.

She turned around and met her husband's hungry gaze. "No."

"Good," he said roughly as he pushed the dress off her shoulders to pool in a puddle of silk at her feet. "Because I am definitely *on edge*."

A fire lit her belly. "Is that a request?"

"Not this time." He brought his palm between her

thighs, seeking out her most intimate flesh. Mina threw back her head as he caressed her in that way that made her crazy.

"It's been too long," she moaned.

"An understatement." He swung her up in his arms, carried her to the bed and brought her down to straddle his thighs. His eyes on hers, he captured her hand and brought it to the zipper that covered the hard bulge beneath his pants, his directive clear.

"Nate—" she breathed, absorbing the pulsing, urgent power of him.

"Shocking—I know," he murmured in her ear. "Do it, anyway."

She did, releasing him and taking him deep inside of her, her fingers curling in his shirt as she rode him to completion, her husband still fully clothed.

"I love you," he murmured against her lips when they finally came up for air. "Even more than I did before."

Her heart dissolved. "Well, that's good," she returned huskily. "Because you promised me forever."

He caught her hand in his, pressing the back of her knuckles to his mouth. "I always follow through on my promises, Signora Brunswick."

So he did. She curled her arms around his neck. "Take me to bed, Signor Brunswick. Before your son wakes me up at some ungodly hour."

He did. Not that he had sleep on his mind.

* * * * *

*If you enjoyed this book,
look out for the last installment of*
THE BILLIONAIRE'S LEGACY:

THE LAST DI SIONE CLAIMS HIS PRIZE
by Maisey Yates

Coming next month.

COMING NEXT MONTH FROM

⊕ HARLEQUIN™

Presents®

Available January 17, 2017

#3497 THE LAST DI SIONE CLAIMS HIS PRIZE
The Billionaire's Legacy
by Maisey Yates
Even unsentimental Alessandro Di Sione can't deny his grandfather's dream of retrieving a scandalous painting. Yet its return depends on outspoken Princess Gabriella. While traveling together to locate the painting, Gabby is drawn to this guilt-ridden man. Could their passion be his salvation?

#3498 THE DESERT KING'S BLACKMAILED BRIDE
Brides for the Taking
by Lynne Graham
Naive Polly Dixon lands in the desert kingdom of Dharia clutching an ornate ring—and finds herself arrested! Carrying the ring has led King Rashad's people to believe that Polly is his long-awaited bride—so Rashad begins a fiery sensual onslaught...

#3499 THE CONSEQUENCE OF HIS VENGEANCE
One Night With Consequences
by Jennie Lucas
Letty Spencer's father once forced her to push away Darius Kyrillos. A decade later, he's come back to claim her. But revenge soon melts into insatiable need. And when Darius discovers his impending fatherhood, he won't allow Letty to dismiss the heat between them...

#3500 BOUGHT TO WEAR THE BILLIONAIRE'S RING
by Cathy Williams
Samantha Wilson never forgot Leo Morgan-White's rejection. But now he'll absolve her mother's debts if Samantha will pose as his fiancée. It won't be long before their agreement comes to an end, but Sam's resistance is buckling under the heat of Leo's expert touch...

HPCNM0117RA

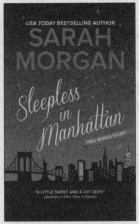

USA TODAY BESTSELLING AUTHOR

SARAH MORGAN

Sleepless in Manhattan

FREE BONUS STORY

"A LITTLE SWEET AND A LOT SEXY."
—*Booklist on First Time in Forever*

$7.99 U.S./$9.99 CAN.

EXCLUSIVE
Limited Time Offer

$1.⁰⁰ OFF

USA TODAY Bestselling Author
SARAH MORGAN

*introduces From Manhattan with Love,
a sparkling new trilogy about three best friends
embracing life—and love—in New York.*

*Paige Walker loves a challenge, but can she
convince a man who trusts no one to take a
chance on forever?*

Sleepless in Manhattan

*Available May 31, 2016.
Pick up your copy today!*

H
HQN™

$1.⁰⁰ OFF

the purchase price of SLEEPLESS IN MANHATTAN by Sarah Morgan.

Offer valid from May 31, 2016, to July 31, 2016. Redeemable at participating retail outlets. Not redeemable at Barnes & Noble. Limit one coupon per purchase. Valid in the U.S.A. and Canada only.

52613760

5 65373 00076 2 (8100)0 12167

® and TM are trademarks owned and used by the trademark owner and/or its licensee.

© 2016 Harlequin Enterprises Limited

PHCOUPSAM0616

Alessandro was so different than she was. Gabby had
never truly fully appreciated just how different men and
women were. In a million ways, big and small.

Yes, there was the obvious, but it was more than that.
And it was those differences that suddenly caused her to
glory in who she was, what she was. To feel, if only for
a moment, that she completely understood herself both
body and soul, and that they were united in one desire.

"Kiss me, Princess," he said, his voice low, strained.

He was affected.

So she had won.

She had been the one to make him burn.

But she'd made a mistake if she'd thought this game
had one winner and one loser. She was right down there
with him. And she didn't care about winning anymore.

She couldn't deny him, not now. Not when he was

looking at her like she was a woman and not a girl, or an owl. Not when he was looking at her like she was the sun, moon and all the stars combined. Bright, brilliant and something that held the power to hold him transfixed.

Something more than what she was. Because Gabriella D'Oro had never transfixed anyone. Not her parents. Not a man.

But he was looking at her like she mattered. She didn't feel like shrinking into a wall or melting into the scenery. She wanted him to keep looking.

She didn't want to hide from this. She wanted all of it.

Slowly, so slowly, so that she could savor the feel of him, relish the sensations of his body beneath her touch, she slid her hand up his throat, feeling the heat of his skin, the faint scratch of whiskers.

Then she moved to cup his jaw, his cheek.

"I've never touched a man like this before," she confessed.

And she wasn't even embarrassed by the confession, because he was still looking at her like he wanted her.

He moved closer, covering her hand with his. She could feel his heart pounding heavily, could sense the tension running through his frame. "I've touched a great many women," he said, his tone grave. "But at the moment it doesn't seem to matter."

That was when she kissed him.

Don't miss
THE LAST DI SIONE CLAIMS HIS PRIZE,
available February 2017 wherever
Harlequin Presents® books and ebooks are sold.

www.Harlequin.com

HARLEQUIN
Presents®

**Don't miss Heidi Rice's thrilling
Harlequin Presents debut—a story of
a couple tempestuously reunited!**

Xanthe Carmichael has just discovered two things:
1. Her ex-husband could take half her business
2. She's actually still married to him!

When she jets off to New York, divorce papers in hand, Xanthe
is prepared for the billionaire bad boy's slick offices…but not for
the spear of lust that hits her the moment she sees Dane Redmond
again! Has her body no shame, no recollection of the pain he
caused? But Dane is stalling… Is he really checking the fine print
or planning to stir the smoldering embers of their passion and
tempt her back into the marriage bed?

Don't miss

*VOWS THEY
CAN'T ESCAPE*
Available February 2017

Stay Connected:

www.Harlequin.com

 /HarlequinBooks

 @HarlequinBooks

 /HarlequinBooks

HP06044